Flat Earth Theory

Flat Earth Theory

Yael Egal

ISBN-13: 9780692619278
ISBN-10: 0692619275

CHAPTER 1

Tess Shapiro sat with her back to the arm of the wheat-colored sectional and stared pensively into the predawn blackness pressing up against the grubby windowpanes. The early-morning, kid-free ritual of having her coffee in solitude was an imperative, and Tess purposefully ignored the detritus from her children that surrounded her: gem-colored magnetic blocks scattered on the brown patterned rug, book bags lying next to unpacked homework, and picture books spilled across the sofa and carpet. Behind her was a conduit of collaged brown butcher paper lining the path between the living and dining areas. It was covered in markers—both capped and uncapped— and seeping bottles of liquid glue.

Though Tess was not a neat freak by nature, this amount of chaos was a bit much even for her, and it was only through clichéd mantras and focused determination that she had learned not to care.

She huffed, and a wisp of dark-blond hair rose off her forehead. Even in the shadowed dimness of early morning, it was possible to see summer's official conclusion—the depletion of giddy happiness that had bathed Brooklyn with its optimistic light and happy adventures for two glorious work-free months. With the start of the school year, and the return to the daily stress of teaching and full frontal parenting, summer already seemed like a half forgotten dream.

Still, Tess pressured herself to welcome autumn's crispness. She reminded herself how it invigorated her, and filled her with romantic feelings, even though it did carry with it the haunting specter of winter. Winter in New York was, for Tess, as dark and shadowy as the wan sheen of light into which she now peered.

And this winter, she reminded herself, would be her first as a single parent. The divorce had been finalized. The papers had arrived by courier and been delivered into her hands by an oblivious doorman as she entered the building with her children, just a few weeks after the start of the school year. There it was, the last ten years of her life compressed into a thick manila folder that might as well have been stamped "fail" in red caps and addressed to someone named "Seriously Stupid and Naive."

Tess shuddered and tried hard not to think of the past year. What had Patrick—lying, cheating Patrick—said as he left? "When I think about the last ten years, I just feel sad."

She should have kept her mouth shut. That's what all her blog reading of stories told by other wives in her situation had taught her: "Do not engage the sociopath. You will not win."

She had hammered the truth of those words into her brain. So why-oh-why had she cried plaintively after him, "What the hell did I ever do to you?"

Dumbass. Sincerely stupid and naïve *dumbass!* Tess chided herself. He had gotten off on that, she knew—gotten off on upsetting her. And she had let it happen.

She swallowed another gulp of coffee and shuddered, willing the memory away. But it was no use. The repressed anger always had to work itself out of her system in the same way. Within moments, she found herself seated at her bedroom desk, the black-domed study light casting a yellow circle on the white-painted wood surface of her desk, onto which she brought a sheaf of blank paper and a newly sharpened pencil.

She peered at the paper for a few moments. What had Hemmingway said? "Until your forehead bleeds." Tess always remembered the quote, but it didn't apply to her. Her stories came from a place of deep self-knowledge—a repressed place. All she had to do was relax, and the words and images belonging to a lifetime of graphic-novel adventures starring Andrea Chambers—the glorious, courageous, and quick-moving international spy who was Tess, but not Tess—took center stage. The pencil began to fly over the page.

CHAPTER 2

PANEL ONE

Andrea Chambers is standing in a windowless cinderblock room. It is cold and she is shivering, holding her arms across her chest for warmth and looking around her worriedly. She is dressed in a pair of black jeans, high heels, and a patterned silk blouse. Above her, a rectangle of Soviet-era fluorescent light is flickering and emitting a *buzz, buzz* sound.

PANEL TWO

A word bubble pointing off-panel to the right contains the exclamation: *Moan!* Andrea swivels to see who is there.

PANEL THREE

In a darkened corner, we see a man tied to a wooden chair with a pillowcase over his head. He is attired in a white button-down shirt, tan trousers, and expensive-looking leather oxfords. Andrea gasps, bringing her French-manicured fingers to her mouth. "Who's there?" she asks.

PANEL FOUR

Before he has a chance to speak, a heavy metal door swings open and two other men walk in. The second man is short, with dark hair plastered to his head and black, horn-rimmed glasses. He is carrying what looks like a shoe box under one arm, but his eyes are focused on the back of the first man, who is tall and familiar to

Andrea. Blue-eyed, white-haired, and handsome, he regards her with repressed mirth. She looks at him, wide eyed, and gasps, "Anton!" Bold exclamations of *Pound, Pound* reverberate around her chest.

PANELS FIVE THROUGH SIX

Anton retrieves a metal folding table that was balanced against a wall and flicks it open with one hand: *Clang!* Then he peers at Andrea with dancing eyes and says, "Hello, Andrea. It is good to see you. It has been some years since I was your sergeant during basic training in Switzerland." Andrea regards him mutely, her face a mask of bravery.

PANELS SEVEN THROUGH EIGHT

The short, dark man deposits his cardboard box on the table and removes the lid with a flourish. Andrea looks at them cautiously before approaching to peer inside. She gasps when she sees what's there.

PANEL NINE

Andrea pulls out of the box a small, square piece of wood with upended nails protruding at regular intervals, like a macabre version of the geo-boards she'd used in math class as a child to make different shapes on with elastic bands.

"What is this for?" She looks at it with a mixture of curiosity and disgust.

PANELS TEN THROUGH ELEVEN

The small dark man walks over to the hooded figure in the chair and removes the pillowcase and gag. Andrea gasps as she recognizes her husband, Jonathan.

He shakes his head and opens his frog-like eyes wide. "Andrea!"

Andrea stares in disbelief. Beside her, Anton says, "You must kill him now."

Andrea looks at him in horror: "I can't kill my husband. I love him! He's the father of my children!"

PANELS TWELVE THROUGH THIRTEEN

Anton shrugs and reaches into the box, pulling out a stack of photographs, and hands them to Andrea. She puts the board of nails on the table to accept them, and her face dissolves into tears. "No, no. It can't be true!" she says as she leafs through the stack of photographs. They fan out in a frozen arc, visible to the reader.

One photo reveals Jonathan at a lounge walled in floor-to-ceiling bookcases. He's reaching under the table to stroke the outer thigh of a blond woman in a black dress. Another shows Jonathan wearing a suit and sitting in a plush red theater seat next to a woman with prominent cheekbones. Next he is seen at a Pan-Asian restaurant with exaggerated ethnic décor, subtly thumbing the nipple of a woman with bobbed red hair.

Holding this photo, Andrea exclaims, "I know her! She's been to our home!"

PANEL FOURTEEN

Andrea pauses at the final photograph and sinks to her knees. In their home, Jonathan stands over a prostitute bent over their dining-room table, thin strings of underwear stretched between her hooker boots.

Anton barks, "*Leve toi!* Get up!"

His face is a mask of disgust.

PANEL FIFTEEN

Slowly, her face set in an expression of hard determination, Andrea raises herself up by gripping the edge of the table.

PANEL SIXTEEN

She picks up the nail board and looks menacingly at Jonathan, who is visibly scared.

He says, "Andrea! Please, no!"

PANEL SEVENTEEN

Andrea stands above Jonathan, the board raised. "No! No!" he cries.

PANELS EIGHTEEN THROUGH NINETEEN

Andrea gathers Jonathan's light brown hair in a bunch and smashes his face into the wooden board: *Crunch!*

When she pulls the board away, Jonathan's face is a mess of blood and flesh, like marinara mixed with noodles of white and blue.

PANEL TWENTY

Andrea lets the board drop to the ground, which is covered by a blue industrial carpet: *Tock!* Blood splatters in a rough circular pattern.

PANEL TWENTY-ONE

Andrea brushes her hands together, nods to them and says, "Gentlemen," and exits.

The emotional exertion of creating, combined with the only partially consumed coffee left behind in the living room, had caused Tess to drift off. Now she felt someone's hand on her head, and she shrieked and jerked it and her body upward.

"Mommy!"

Rosie jumped back, startled, holding her hand as if stung. Tess gasped, wide eyed, searching for the alarm clock.

"Jesus, it's 7:20!"

Rosie looked contrite. "I know. I came to get you. Sammy is making breakfast."

"Oh God."

"It's okay, I told him not to stick his hand in the toaster oven again." Rosie looked down and reached for one of the pages on Tess's desk. "Mommy, what is this?"

But Tess grabbed them soundlessly and pushed them into her desk drawer and then leaped to her feet and scurried toward the kitchen, Rosie quick on her heels. Gray light now paled outside the windows, and either Sammy or Rosie—she guessed Sammy—had turned on each and every light. The smell of burned toast seemed ominously close to the "smoke detector about to go off" end of the spectrum.

In the kitchen alcove, just off the dining area, Sammy stood on a small white Ikea stool in front of the black granite countertop, sloshing milk over the sides of a cereal bowl as the toaster pinged. An impressive pile of already incinerated bread sat on the cutting board in front of it. Tess clutched her hair and forced herself to speak calmly.

"Sammy, sweetheart, Mommy made a big boo-boo. I didn't wake up on time, and now we have to really hurry up or you'll be late for school, and I'll be late for work."

He looked at her suspiciously, and she took a deep breath before continuing.

"Listen, just for today, I need both you guys to eat school breakfast and lunch, okay? And not argue with me while getting ready?"

"No!"

"Hmm, that's too bad. Because I was thinking that after I pick you up, I could make it up to you by taking you to Dunkin' Donuts." She could see his resolve weakening as he pursed his lips and looked sideways. "*And* an ice cream cone."

"Okay."

"Yay!" Rosie bounded into her room.

"I'm going to be ready first!"

"No, you're not!" Sammy stormed into his room and banged the door shut.

Tess felt a rush of relief. "Let's make it a race. Winner gets *two* scoops of ice cream!"

Mentally she added, *And I get the Mother of the Year award!*

CHAPTER 3

Tess urged her children to walk faster as they trudged, oblivious to her anxiety, up Smith Street, past the vacant lot bordering the notoriously polluted Gowanus Canal, and around the cement factories that were just activating their grinding and humming mechanisms. The walk finally ended at the steps leading up to the blue-painted metal door of the school cafeteria at PS 30. Here, Tess bid her children a hurried good-bye, kissing them hard on each of their cheeks.

"I love you!" she called, as they scrambled up the steps.

"Love you more." Rosie paused halfway up the steps to blow her a final kiss, her straight brown hair swinging against her denim jacket.

Tess turned and sighed, the tension ebbing out of her. She glanced at her watch. By some miracle of time management, she still had twenty minutes to go, and her own school was only a block and a half away. She turned and made her way up President Street toward Carroll Park, keeping her strides quick and even, but letting herself relax both mentally and physically before the vigor of the day.

Landing a position as a the fifth-grade General Studies teacher in the bilingual French program at PS 52 had been an amazing stroke of luck, she knew, and Tess didn't want to do anything to jeopardize her job. She knew she had only gotten it because she spoke French passably well, giving her an advantage over other, probably younger candidates. But they would have had difficulty communicating with the children of recent immigrants, and Tess could get by in this regard, thanks to the year she had spent at a Canadian junior college in Switzerland, the year after high school.

She took a deep, cleansing breath and felt uplifted by the explosion of beauty at this end of the neighborhood. The brown and gray Victorian stone homes were fronted by large, impressively cultivated gardens, which had led to the area being dubbed "Carroll Gardens." Tess savored the evergreen smell, which reminded her of her childhood home of Vancouver, Canada, although it was a shallow echo of the intense natural beauty she had been surrounded by in her youth.

But the architecture, she thought as she neared Smith Street—the whole hipster-affected, Victorian vibe of the neighborhood she now lived in—was far more reminiscent of Toronto, where she had gone to university and teachers' college.

She sighed as she skirted the eastern edge of Carroll Park. The sidewalks were bustling with commuters heading toward the subway stairs with paper coffee cups in hand, and parents tugging their children to school. Her own school now visible, she quickened her steps, her black clogs scuffing rhythmically. Unconsciously, she drew her index finger under each eye to collect any smear of black liner that might have pooled there from perspiring on her hurried walk.

She wasn't really sure why she bothered with makeup for a teaching job, except that her mother had always emphasized the importance of personal appearance. That and finding a sport that would prevent her from ever getting fat. After Tess had failed miserably at everything else, they had finally landed on figure skating, which at least Tess had enjoyed, and still did.

She reached the corner at the same time as a family with two children. Neither of them was in her class, but they smiled up at her, offering tiny waves of recognition. The white-capped crossing guard looked pinch faced as she heralded them across, a departure from her usual, cheerful demeanor. Tess wondered if something had happened, but then, as she reached the other side of the street, she saw parents gathered like twittering hummingbirds around a particularly succulent hydrangea in the center of the school yard.

She lengthened her strides, curious. On a spot of higher incline half-way up the sidewalk, Tess gripped the chain-link fence and raised herself on tiptoe, straining to see. Just then, a couple turned away, shaking their heads and speaking in loud, outraged voices.

"C'est pas possible!"

Thin and impeccably clad in skinny jeans and a black faux-fur vest, the woman stared pensively at the ground as she walked.

Her equally fashion-conscious husband kicked at a stone with a pointed leather toe. *"Qui pourrait faire une telle chose terrible?"*

Tess peered at the spot they had just vacated, desperate to see what "terrible thing" they were referring to. All the heat ran out of her as she saw the object of all the attention.

Someone had spray-painted a large white circle on the asphalt and lettered within: Go Home French People!

CHAPTER 4

The children sat in a large circle on the bright blue rug, facing Tess and her partner, Aleksia. Although Aleksia normally taught in the adjacent French-language room, as the children alternated classrooms every day, now the two of them sat on low chairs next to the high windows overlooking the school yard, both classes gathered together. Bright sunlight shafted into Tess's eyes, and she scooted her chair a little to avoid it, taking refuge in one of the patches of shade made by the projects hung in front of the windows.

Aleksia was Canadian also, but French and from Montreal. Her disdain for Tess's lack of fluency was apparent now, as she arched her thin brows and pouted her full lips. In general, she acted as though Tess embodied every aspect of the French-English conflict in Canada, and it was her personal affliction to suffer being partnered with such a dreary encumbrance.

Apparently, it was Tess who needed to start the conversation with the children. She fiddled with the braided leather bracelet she wore and cleared her throat. Forty-six faces looked at her expectantly.

Must get this right, she thought. Although she knew that no matter what she said, it would be repeated at home, and some parent or another would take offense and either call the principal or write a nasty note. Despite years of teaching, she had never quite become accustomed to these surprise attacks, which always left her feeling like she had been punched in the gut.

She took a deep breath and began. "Okay, so is there anyone in the class who did not see or hear about the not-nice message that was painted in our school yard this morning?"

A chorus of no's and *non*'s rumbled through the assembly, and Tess nodded and assumed a grave expression.

"Well, I know it's very hard to understand how someone could do something like that, but you know when people do nasty things it's for... why? Why do people act unkindly?"

A boy small boy named Michael, who made up for his lack of stature with a thick tangle of uncombed black hair, arched his back as he raised his hand. "Because they're sad inside?" he offered.

Tess nodded. "Yes, people do unkind things sometimes, but we always need to keep in mind that if they were happy with life, and happy with themselves, they wouldn't try and make other people feel bad."

A beautiful girl named Ashley, with cornflower-blue eyes and golden hair tied back in braids, raised her hand next. "It's because they want other people to be unhappy like them, right? We need to try and be nice to them."

Tess nodded. She felt pleased and proud. Her kindness sermons during circle time had not fallen on deaf ears. Then she turned to Aleksia.

"That's very wise, don't you agree, Aleksia?"

Aleksia shrugged. "It is unfortunate sometimes French people elicit this feeling. People are jealous of us."

Tess gaped at her in horror. "I'm sure Aleksia doesn't mean..."

But she could feel the circle ripple with disillusionment, like a delicately constructed edifice rocked by an earthquake.

She opened her mouth but was interrupted by a light tapping at the door. All forty-eight heads swiveled in unison to see Principal White, an expectant smile on her face, accompanied by a small boy with an auburn ponytail and the most gorgeous man Tess had ever laid eyes upon.

Tall and sinewy in jeans and a dark brown leather jacket that hung from perfectly angled shoulders, he also wore his hair in a ponytail, only his was steely gray. This did nothing to diminish the piercing luminosity of his blue-green eyes, which peered at her over high cheekbones, in a way that made Tess flush hotly. It was with difficulty that she managed to arrange her features in a professional teacher's smile, resisting the impulse to run a smoothing hand over her hair.

Principal White spoke. "Tess, Aleksia, and children: This is Yves."

She indicated the little boy with upturned palms, her large white teeth bared in a smile to disguise what Tess intuited was stress from the morning's graffiti incident. Her normally perfect blond bob showed signs of disarray, and her pink neckerchief was twisted so that the knot had slid to the base of her throat.

The class chorused, "Hello, Yves," and Tess smiled at the boy, who was flushing with embarrassment. His eyes, carbon copies of his father's, were wide and staring. He wore navy-blue sweatpants, the cuffs of which were a bit too short and revealed subtly mismatched white sweat socks. It drifted through Tess's mind that his father must have helped him pick out what to wear that morning. A mother would make sure that for the first day at a new school her son was well attired. Perhaps, she thought fleetingly, Yves's father was single.

Aleksia spoke to Yves in French. *"Venez et rejoignez le cercle yves. Nous sommes heureux de vous accueillir."*

His father smiled and gave Yves a gentle push of encouragement. Yves walked with his head down—the tops of his ears pink—toward the circle of children on the rug, circumventing the clusters of desks with book bags hung across their chairs. The children stared in silence. Only the squeak of his blue Converse sneakers could be heard on the blond-tiled linoleum.

Later that day, Tess leaned over Yves's desk to help him understand the English directions in his math workbook. She couldn't help but be impressed by his obvious intelligence. Once he understood the directions, his pencil raced over the page, solving the decimal equations without him once reaching for a piece of scratch paper.

Tess smiled and asked him in French, "Did your mother travel with you here to New York?"

Yves shook his head. *"Elle est morte,"* he said simply.

The emotionless way in which he stated the fact of his mother's death made Tess's stomach spasm with a mixture of shock and projected fear.

CHAPTER 5

Aleksia had learned that Yves's father's name was Guy. She had also learned that he was a widower, his wife having apparently committed suicide during an untreated or undiagnosed bout of postnatal depression. She imparted this information to Tess offhandedly, dropping by Tess's classroom after school one day. Leaning casually against the door frame, she stood with her ankles crossed and arms folded over her chest. She shrugged at the end of her story.

"He chose life, *enfin*," she finished.

Tess paused her straightening to listen, working hard to keep her expression free of any nonprofessional interest—or abhorrence for Aleksia's lack of compassion. In truth, the concept of committing suicide after a child was born was almost unfathomable to her, no matter how many magazine articles featuring celebrities suffering from the condition she read, and she felt for the man and the child she hardly knew.

The sadness of it occupied her thoughts as she walked over to pick up her own children from the free afterschool program at their school. She imagined a younger-looking Guy entering a bohemian Paris apartment, calling to his wife, hearing the baby's cries and then—!

She shuddered, hugging her own children extra tightly when they flung themselves on her in the school lobby.

Later that night, after a hasty supper of hamburgers, sliced carrots, and cucumbers (some of which—she suspected Sammy's—she later found buried under some toilet tissue in the bathroom trash can), and after homework, showers and stories, Tess poured herself a large glass of white wine and flopped down on the sofa, flipping on the television set. New York One flickered onto the screen, and she was ready to see what she had recorded on the DVR, when the broadcast changed over to international news.

The screen filled with images of streams of Arab refugees, seeking—according to the voice-over reporter—political asylum in France. The male voice spoke with a British accent.

"The mostly Christian Arabs, from countries including Algeria, Lebanon, Morocco and Syria, are seeking asylum from a slew of terrorists attacks by Islamic extremists, which has been plaguing the region for months."

The footage switched over to a woman in a red patterned head scarf, clutching a small boy, pleading with whoever was interviewing her. The British reporter translated: "They are bombing our schools, our churches—even cafés frequented by Christians have been the target of terrorist attacks. We are pleading with the French government. You came to our country. You conquered, you ruled. We took your language and religion. Now you must repay us. You must let us come live in France."

Tess sat up and shuddered, looking at the crying child. When she was younger, she had read the paper or watched the news every day. Since her own children had been born, however, she had avoided it like the plague. Somehow, the sufferings of others now resonated with her as the suffering of someone's son, daughter, mother, or father.

For this reason, Al Queda or ISIS terrorism being directed against fellow Arabs in the Middle East—Arabs who happened to be Christian—was news to her. She hoped France would do the right thing and remembered her own feelings after 9/11, wondering when and where the next attack would occur. She hadn't been a parent then, but if she had, she wondered how she would have dealt with the constant stress and worry of it.

She chewed her lip and drew her knees up to her chest, her wine glass balanced in one hand as she stared unseeingly at the bookshelf beneath the television; thinking about the day terrorism came to America.

She had been teaching in a Jewish day school on the Upper West Side at the time, winding down in her relationship with the boyfriend she had come to New York with. At first she had been thrilled when he asked her to accompany her to the Big Apple for a one year work commitment offered to him by the bank he worked for, but living together had proved to be too much of a strain on their relationship. This had already become apparent, Tess remembered, by that fateful day. Tess remembered every moment of it—the sirens, the school on lockdown, going out onto the roof with the custodian to see the helicopters, and the bits of information gleaned online while the children were out of the classrooms for art or gym.

Then, at the end of the day, she remembered the parents coming to pick up their children, their faces masks of shock, horror, and disbelief. Their arms seemed to quake as they reached to embrace their offspring.

When the final parent had come and gone, she stood at the entranceway near the Israeli security guard and the elevators, staring out at the eerily quiet and sunny afternoon. A Hebrew teacher came and pushed the up button on the elevator. While Tess waited, the teacher conversed with the guard in Hebrew. But Tess, whose memory of the language from her own Jewish-day-school days had returned since working there, found she was able to understand.

The teacher said, "Now the world will see what they are."

The security guard nodded in agreement and tapped the pen he was holding on the podium he sat behind.

"The Muslims! Yes, that's right. Now they'll understand."

Tess stared at the floor. A glut of revulsion churned inside her, and she didn't want them to see it on her face.

Just then the principal, a disheveled, bohemian woman in her fifties—Karen White's polar opposite—had appeared, full of hugs and emotive proclamations. In response, Tess had mumbled something original like, "Well, I guess we'll always remember where we were on this day," which had moved the poor woman to tears.

Embarrassed, Tess had left the building without going back upstairs to straighten her room or retrieve her sweater. As she walked slowly home, past the dazed New Yorkers—the stores rolling down their metal gates, the restaurants and coffee shops seeming patriotic and somehow defiant by staying open—she realized that something about her had changed. She didn't quite understand what, but it was shortly after that that she began dating Patrick—as un-Jewish as they come, with Southern roots and a preacher father. She, Tess Shapiro. He was the first non-Jew she had ever dated, and she married him.

Behind the sofa was another bookshelf of cubbies filled with the children's things, including art supplies, paper, and pencils. Tess got up and grabbed a sheaf of blank paper, a pencil, and a board book to balance on her knees as she resumed her position on the sofa and began to draw.

PANEL ONE
Caption: "The oldest synagogue in Lausanne is a simmering heap of ash and debris."

We see a collapsed, smoking building. Piles of bricks, shattered glass, and dirt fill the frame.

PANEL TWO
Dressed in white pants and a black blazer, her black bobbed hair pulled back in a white hair tie, Andrea sits at a table in a hotel conference room across from an elderly Swiss woman.

The elderly woman, attired in a floral dress and sensible shoes, her black handbag clasped on her lap, speaks to Andrea in French: "Je veux finir mes jours en Israel." ["I want to finish my days in Israel."]

In the corner of the room behind Andrea, an Israeli flag is draped across a wall, next to a television set with ongoing coverage of the terror incident. A reporter is indicating a procession of survivors and saying: "These are the latest victims of an Al Qaeda attack on a Swiss synagogue, which comes just days after a fire bomb exploded in a Jewish museum. Fortunately that attack happened on a Saturday, when the facility was closed."

PANEL THREE
The elderly woman has tears in her eyes: "I wish I would have left sooner. Europe is a graveyard for the Jews. I am happy that the Swiss government is working together with Israel to allow us to emigrate."

Andrea responds: "I'm not actually Israeli, you know. I'm Canadian, but I've been to Israel. It's a beautiful place. You will like it there, and we will do everything we can to make it a smooth transition for you."

PANEL FOUR
The woman leans forward. "If you are not Swiss and not Israeli, what are you doing here?"

Andrea responds: "I sometimes do work on behalf of the Swiss government."

PANEL FIVE
The woman's eyes become wide, and she points at the television set behind Andrea. *"Je remercie Dieu pour ces bénévoles, mais je parie que c'est dangereux."* ["I'm grateful for the work of these volunteers, but I fear it may be dangerous."]

PANEL SIX
Andrea swivels to see. A female reporter is interviewing a familiar-looking man. It takes Andrea a moment to realize it is Jonathan, as he is covered in sweat and smears of dirt, and his hair is coated in white dust.

"Jonathan!" she exclaims.

PANEL SEVEN

The woman looks at Andrea with surprise: "You know this man?" Andrea nods. "He's my husband, but he's supposed to be watching the children!"

PANEL EIGHT

The woman says, "You must go find them. You must not leave your children."

Andrea stands. "Never! I would never leave them. I'm so sorry but we will have to continue this conversation after lunch."

PANEL NINE

The woman nods and touches Andrea's arm. "I understand."

CHAPTER 6

Tess's comic-book spy fantasies dated back to childhood. It was her way, she reflected, as she placed her latest installment into the wooden chest in her bedroom, of escaping.

While Tess had been a struggling math student in middle school, Andrea Chambers had been an undercover spy who kept a pistol hidden in her strawberry-festooned binder. When a group of Russian agents burst into Tess's classroom moments before the midterm exam, Andrea had shot them dead before anyone had a chance to react. While Tess had worked hard to penetrate the groups of gossiping girls outside of school, Andrea Chambers had been whisked away by a flag-bearing black limousine that screeched to a stop in front of Tess's school building. Where Tess was socially awkward and physically weak, Andrea Chambers was a sophisticated martial-arts expert, and always fashionable. And unlike Tess, Andrea Chambers was proud of being different.

Because Tess was different. In some ways, she thought, peering into her gray-blue eyes in the mirror above the dresser, it was good. It was as if she saw life at a slant, perceived things that others were oblivious to. Like when Karen Kutler had her sleepover birthday party in the seventh grade, and they were playing Truth or Dare, huddled in their sleeping bags on the white carpet of Karen's rec room.

Tess knew Karen was going to repeat everything everyone said to the boys at school on Monday. Only nobody else seemed to know. Everyone else was surprised and mad, and Karen wound up having to switch to the public school near her house after everyone she betrayed made her life a living hell. But Tess had looked into Karen's eyes and had known what she was going to do, even if the "why" eluded her.

It was an advantage, she thought, to be able to see through things and people, to perceive the truth that others were unwilling, or unable, to accept. But then why hadn't she seen through Patrick? What had blinded her? Fear, she now thought. She had sensed, without realizing it, that a temper lurked beneath the façade of reasonableness.

She huffed, pulled off her clothes, and put on a pair of plaid cotton pajamas before crawling beneath the covers. Hands clasped behind her head, she stared at the ceiling and thought glumly that the other ways in which she had always differed from her peers were not advantages at all. They were unquestionably deficiencies—then and now.

Tess was awkward socially and tried to compensate by imitating girls she deemed socially perfect. The problem was she didn't always get it right. How, she wondered, did the other girls know that sixth grade was the year you no longer gave Valentine's Day cards to the boys—just your female friends? Tess had already given hers out by the time she realized this and was mortified. It didn't help that she could tell some of the boys were happy to get a Valentine from her—that they glanced from it to her with softness in their eyes.

She punched her pillow but did not close her eyes. Instead she frowned at the wall, angry at herself for working herself up into this funk. Perhaps, she thought, the comics really prevented her from facing up to her demons. Rather than coming to terms with things, she escaped through her alter ego.

She remembered how it had all started. Her mother, the community cheerleader, was organizing for the annual Hadassah Bazar fundraiser. It was being held in a giant warehouse, and all the kids were running around while the mothers sifted through piles of donated clothing, books, and housewares, and set up their booths. It was at the booth for secondhand books where Tess discovered the pile of '60s romance comic books. Furtively, she gathered them up and hid behind a rack of ladies' dresses, immersing herself in the captivating drawings and - for ten-year-old Tess - enlightening story lines.

Hours later, she had heard her parents' calls echoing frantically through the almost-emptied-out space. She had read throughout the entire evening and crawled out sheepishly from her hiding place, her new passion and lifetime obsession slipping from her arms like water from an overfull sponge. Fortunately, they had embraced her and greeted her with exclamations of relief and gratitude, instead of reprimands.

And that was how Tess remembered her parents: loving, normal, supportive. So what had happened to her mother after her father passed away from prostate cancer at the start of Tess's final year of high school? Within a few months, she turned into a maniacal spendthrift, spending her days in shopping malls and furniture stores like a suddenly cured anorexic released into a bakery.

And then she had insisted that Tess defer her acceptance to the University of Toronto and attend some exclusive school for Canadians in Switzerland, only announcing days after Tess's landing in that foreign country that she herself was moving to Toronto!

Tess groaned and rolled over, finally sitting up and turning on the light. She should just get up, she thought. Then the phone rang. She padded out to the living room, thinking it was probably a good thing she hadn't fallen asleep after all, because it was probably a sales call and she would've been so angry that it would've taken her hours to fall back asleep again.

When she saw the 416 area code, however, she didn't bother to look at the rest of the number. She picked up the phone.

"Mom?"

There was a pause. "No…Tess? Is that you?"

Tess released a breathy chortle. "Courtney? Yes! Is that you?"

Her old friend and roommate from the year she'd lived in Switzerland gushed through the phone. She still spoke with the same melodic air of someone who was breathlessly enthusiastic about pretty much everything, but in the years since they'd downgraded their friendship to Facebook chats and comments, her voice had deepened somewhat—and now contained an air of alarm.

"Oh God, I'm so sorry! I've been meaning to call or write. I saw you changed your name on Facebook back to Shapiro. Did you…does that mean…?"

Tess sighed and lowered her voice. "That I'm divorced? Yes. I'm sorry too—it took me forever to be able to even say it, or talk about it. I would have written, but it was the most horrible year ever."

She sat down with her back to the sofa, biting her lip and bracing herself for the roll call of sympathy-card sentences she knew were to follow. She was surprised when Courtney was at a loss for words.

After a few minutes of gaping silence, she said, "Tess, what happened? You guys looked so happy together!"

Tess took a deep breath and repeated the same story for the thousandth time. When she was finished, she could tell from the dead-line silence that Courtney was well and truly shocked. Tess squeezed her eyes shut, waiting.

Finally Courtney's voice burst the void. "I mean, *Patrick?* Of all people, he just does not seem the type. Hookers? In the *apartment?* My God!"

"I know. I know."

Tess's eyes darted around the dimly lit room, searching for her iPhone. It was not on the charger, but she found it on the coffee table. She scrolled through her Facebook friends until she found Courtney and clicked on her profile picture. For some reason she felt compelled to see her friend's face as they spoke. It had been so long.

Courtney said, "And how is it now, between you guys? I mean, do you get along or fight or…?"

Tess sighed. "I guess 'polite but formal' would best describe it. I can't look at him. It gives me nightmares. Literally."

Tess shuddered, thinking of the nights she'd woken up in a cold sweat, gasping. The funny thing was that the dreams were all about rodents; some were disguised as cute, fluffy pets. In the dreams, only Tess knew they were actually rodents, and she tried to warn people but found she couldn't speak.

She continued, "I offered him friendship, but he just turned into this cruel monster. He's really sick."

"Yeah! God!"

There was another silence.

Courtney said, "Hey Tess? I'm sorry to change the subject, but do you remember that museum in Lausanne we used to go to? I mean the one I used to drag you to? La Musee Cantonal des Beux Arts?"

Tess smiled, remembering. Courtney, a former art major who now sat on the board of directors at the Royal Ontario Museum, had often coerced Tess into taking the train with her to Lausanne to go to the museums and look at paintings and sculpture. Unlike Tess, Courtney loved "high art." Tess could take it for about an hour, but the sort of art revered as priceless works by masters was as lost on her as the goose-liver pâté and caviar at Union Market - a high-end gourmet food shop in her neighborhood - and she mostly looked forward to their excursions afterward: rowing on the lake, walking through the shops, and eating at the outdoor cafés. Then, as dusk fell, they would take exhausted train rides home; trundling peacefully through the idyllic countryside, Tess with her forehead pressed up against the glass, as villages and mountains sped past.

"Of course I remember," she said. "That building is so beautiful. I actually didn't mind going to that one."

"Tess—it's been bombed. I just heard it on the news."

"What?" Tess sat bolt upright, her heart racing, and then went over the computer. She shook the mouse violently and tapped on the space bar to wake it up. Then she clicked on CNN—and brought her hand to her mouth. Sure enough, there was the old stone building, half collapsed, singed and smoking.

"Jesus," she said. "I'm looking at it now. What happened?"

Courtney sounded as though she were speaking through tears. "They had just got this installation of French art. Well, it's a little fishy because it was art that was probably stolen from Jews during World War Two, so there was actually a lot of chatter and controversy about it in the art world. But anyway, it went up yesterday, and today the whole museum was detonated by dynamite or something."

"Who did it?"

"Some German-national group of crazies calling themselves NAFKA. The National Aryan Front for Kindred Affairs, or something?"

"Aryan?"

"I know."

"My God, what the hell do they want?"

Sweat pooled under Tess's armpits and trickled down the insides of her pajama top. She passed the back of her sleeve over the gleam of perspiration that beaded over her forehead before walking over to the window and yanking it open, the phone scrunched between her shoulder and ear. A waft of cool night air settled over her. On the other end of the line, she heard a sniffle and nose-blow.

Courtney's voice trembled. "Who the hell knows? I mean, I think they're pissed off with the French economy and the way they're taking over Europe and everything. It's down to the euro again, I think."

Tess shook her head, disbelieving. "Terrorists! They're just fucking terrorists."

Courtney sniffed. "That's what they're saying, yeah. Gosh, I haven't been there in a hundred years, but I'm going to miss that place."

Tess's voice came full of breath. "Me too."

CHAPTER 7

Courtney. How long had it been? Twenty years? Tess sat at her desk, a pile of uncorrected math tests in front of her, while the children were at P.E. Absently, she twirled a red pen between her fingers and gazed out the window, lost in reminiscence.

She could have chosen anyone, but Courtney had asked Tess to be her roommate that year, and they'd had so much fun together—mostly by breaking all the rules and sneaking out of the house they were boarded at, or cutting class and going on train rides like the ones to Lausanne.

When spring had finally come that year, after a long, cold winter, they had refused to waste the beautiful afternoons cooped up, doing homework. Instead, they sought out boys and adventure. During lunch hour, they made excuses not to return to their pension for lunch as they were supposed to, and instead ate at the cafés in town, flouncing into the common room with minutes to go before class, to get their homework done.

It was on one such fine day that they had come into the deserted, maroon-walled room, with French doors open onto the balcony overlooking the town and the lake. Someone had left two neatly stacked piles of identical pamphlets in the middle of the highly polished wooden table, and Courtney reached over to grab one as Tess hurriedly pulled her geography textbook and binder out of her school bag. She had just turned to the questions at the end of the chapter to see if she could answer them without having read it, when Courtney dropped a pamphlet onto her book, blocking her view.

She groaned but picked it up grudgingly. It was glossy and folded horizontally like a map. On each section were pictures of young people dressed in army uniforms. They wore machine guns slung across their backs as they trekked through picturesque meadows, lush with purple wildflowers, the majestic, snowcapped Alps in the background.

The heading at the top said *Salvia,* and beneath the photograph a caption read: "Named for the purple flowers that blanket the meadows of the Alps during the spring and summer months, this program offers a once-in-a-lifetime opportunity for young people to become familiar with an important Swiss rite of passage."

Other photographs featured smiling uniformed youths with mud smeared on their faces, engaging in target practice and pitching green army tents.

Tess had scoffed and pushed the pamphlet aside before turning her attention to her homework, but Courtney had gushed with enthusiasm, "Oh, Tess, we have to do this!"

Tess hadn't answered but rather had begun writing frenzied, halfbaked answers in her binder. Soon, however, her stomach twinged uneasily as Courtney's eyes bore into her.

"The army!" Tess said. "Are you kidding me? Come on, Courtney. I'd die! You know I would."

Courtney had waved a hand. "Oh, you will not! They're not going to ask you to do anything you aren't capable of. And anyway, if you can't do it, then you can't do it. What are they going to do, make you?"

"My understanding of the military, as a concept, is that yes, that is exactly what they do."

But Courtney had continued to read, a glow of enthusiasm radiating from her, oblivious to Tess's rising panic. Of course, Tess had thought, it would be easy enough for Courtney. She took ski hills like a stallion and returned bullet-speed tennis balls without breaking a sweat. Courtney was, in Tess's opinion, physically impeachable. But Tess could barely run three blocks. She didn't think she could do a single push-up if her life depended on it.

She shook her head, gathered her school books, and rose. "No way. Just forget it, Courtney."

But Courtney wouldn't forget it. She kept hounding Tess for days until finally, Tess relented.

She remembered Courtney's cheer and cheek-pressed hug. Tess's stomach had been in knots, but she'd felt a wash of pleasure at having made her friend so happy.

But then, a few weeks later, on a particularly warm afternoon when both girls had decided to spend their Saturday afternoon in town, Courtney had met Gilles. They were seated outside, under the red-and-white-striped awning of Café Centreville in downtown Neuchatel. Around them, shoppers and strollers basked with obvious delight in the perfect weather, chatting amiably and peering up occasionally at the crystal-blue sky, as if it was the first time they'd ever set eyes upon it.

They had ordered the warm beer favored by the Swiss and an order of French fries to share. Tess remembered how happy she had felt. Then she had spotted a handsome young man, dressed in jean shorts and a black Pearl Jam T-shirt, making his way to their table. She froze and kicked her friend under the table. Tess could still remember his confident smile and shining brown eyes, focused not on her, but on Courtney, as he approached them. She watched, deflated, as he introduced himself to her friend with smooth assurance. Within moments he had her number, and within a month Courtney had become enmeshed in a romance that left Tess feeling bereft and abandoned.

Then, one day after they had already got their acceptance letters and instructions from the Swiss Army, Courtney had dropped the bomb: she and Gilles were going to spend the summer travelling together. She was *so* sorry, and of course she understood if Tess never spoke to her again (which Tess was of a mind never to do), and anyway Tess still had her return ticket to Toronto, right? She hadn't changed it yet?

She had. Tess supposed she could change it back, but what was the point? Courtney had been right when she said Tess would have a miserable summer by herself in Toronto, and besides, she had spent the past two months psyching herself up, getting used to the idea. It would be fun. It would be an experience of a lifetime. She would make new friends. She wouldn't regret it.

Now, Tess sighed and got up from her desk to yank open the class-room window, taking deep pulls of fresh air. The end of September brought with it an eruption of fiery-colored leaves, orange-tinted late-afternoon skies, and air that smelled like wafts of campfire smoke and aged barrels of wine.

As much as she loved the season, it reminded Tess achingly of the breathtaking beauty of Canadian autumns, where nature was more rugged and roughhewn. She had grown up surrounded by jagged mountains and streets littered with colorful leaves, their rich scent imbibing her and, without her realizing it, providing the spiritual decanter into which the religion of her youth had been poured. Without it, Tess had no feelings of God or religion, but she knew her upbringing was the veil through which she viewed the world.

Sounds of the children ambling up the stairs snapped her out of her reverie. She went out into the hallway to greet them.

"I want to see everyone line up nicely before we go inside," she instructed, tapping the wall and mouthing, "Thank you," to Mr. Franks, the P.E. teacher. After a few moments, they quieted down and Tess instructed them to go quietly into the room and take out their handwriting books.

"It's independent worktime until dismissal," she said. "I'll come around and check on you as you work."

The children filed in and Tess cast a penitent eye at the math papers. She had wasted her time and would have to correct them at home. Karen would have something to say if she came in and saw her working at her desk instead of circulating.

The children were busy with their cursive workbooks when suddenly the nurse appeared at her door looking frazzled and out of breath. She put her hand to her ample bosom and said, "Lice check! Sorry I'm so late."

Tess nodded knowingly, as if she had been expecting her. In fact, she hadn't checked her work e-mail that day but clapped her hands to get the class' attention, as if the coming of this event had been well established.

"Everyone, there's a quick lice check before dismissal. We'll call you out one by one, okay?"

She pulled an extra chair into the hallway and gave the nurse, a short but thickly set woman with ruddy cheeks and a thin halo of black curls, a reassuring smile. She nodded in return and rolled her eyes at her own scattiness as she snapped on a pair of blue latex gloves.

Tess addressed the class again. "*A*s first! Adele?"

A red-haired girl with blue eyes and freckles walked submissively into the hallway. Tess checked her watch and calculated. She would need to get them packed up in ten minutes. Fortunately, Nurse Sanders seemed to have collected herself and was flicking through their heads with two unsharpened pencils like a well-oiled machine. Only a little more than ten minutes later, she had checked the whole class. She appeared at Tess's side as she supervised their packing up, a look of horror on her face.

She pointed at Yves. Tess bit her lip and raised her eyebrows knowingly.

"I've never seen such lice," the nurse proclaimed in a stage whisper, her hand turned sideways against her mouth.

Tess sighed. "It's dismissal now. There's no point in sending him to the office. I'll tell his sitter at pickup. Do you have the form?"

Nurse Sanders handed her the regulation slip, which proclaimed in bold: children will not be readmitted to class until they have been cleared for lice and nits. Yves's sitter was from Senegal and didn't speak much English, but Tess supposed she could manage with her French and a healthy dose of pantomime.

Outside, the sun was bright and the air warm. The usual collage of socially adroit fashionistas chatted with amiable self-awareness as they waited for their children's classes to snake through the throngs of adults to their line-up spots. People now scuffed over the black-washed graffiti unthinkingly, the incident assimilated and forgotten.

Since Courtney's call, Tess had avoided the news as usual, except to scan the headlines on Google News. She could not bear to read the full articles, as more and more attacks on Christian Arabs in the Middle East included daycares, universities, and even, horrifically, a school bus, with twenty-two nine-year-olds burned alive on their way home.

Silently, she eyed the French parents in her class at pickup time, wondering what their thoughts were regarding their country's refusal to accept more than a trickle of immigrants from Northern Africa, remembering what the Canadian immigration minister had said when asked how many Jewish refugees he would accept from Nazi Germany: "None is too many."

The crowd thinned, and Tess regarded her two remaining students: Michael and Yves. Suddenly she remembered: "Michael, don't you have an after-school activity on Thursdays?"

Michael flushed. "I have basketball!"

Tess laughed. "Okay, just go back in through the cafeteria entrance."

Michael took off like a shot, his frayed Avengers schoolbag swinging like a pendulum on his back as he ran. Just then Tess felt the hairs on her neck furl, and she swiveled to see Guy approaching, regarding them with hooded eyes, his chin dipped. He sauntered indulgently, as if he never hurried and thought it rather humorous that other people bothered to do so.

Tess put forward her most professional teacher's smile. "How are you?"

Guy's mouth twitched as Yves hurled himself into his father's arms and began babbling in French. Tess took a deep breath.

"I think he was worried."

Guy nodded and squeezed his eyes shut as he hugged his son. Tess's stomach gave a tiny flutter. Then she remembered. She cleared her throat. "Listen, I'm so sorry to have to tell you, but Yves has lice. You're going to have to get rid of them tonight. Otherwise they won't let him back to class in the morning."

She handed him Nurse Sanders' slip and watched as Guy's relaxed expression crumpled. He looked like he was about to be sick. Tess opened her eyes wide with alarm.

"Are you okay?"

Guy brought his fist to his mouth and nodded unconvincingly as his cheeks bulged. Yves stared at him with an expression that mirrored the alarm Tess felt. Guy muttered something to Yves in French, and he nodded again, biting his lip and staring at the ground, his cheeks pink.

Then Yves looked up—and Tess saw with surprise that he was repressing laughter.

"It is my father," he said. Tess was amazed by how well he could speak English already! "He does not like crawling things."

Yves made a motion with his fingers, like a bug crawling up his forearm, and then laughed heartily. Tess couldn't help but break out into a big smile, but Guy looked at him admonishingly and recovered his cool veneer.

He sighed. "It's just that, we are so new here. I do not know what products to buy or how to take care of this."

Tess thought, "Nice save," but nodded gravely and adjusted her smile to one of helpfulness.

"It's really easy," she explained. "Well, at least the first part is. You can buy the products for Yves's hair right over there at the Rite Aid."

She pointed to the corner building on the other side of the park. Its brick exterior was lined with large panes of glass displaying indispensable decorations and housewares for Halloween and Thanksgiving.

"That will be enough for him to pass inspection tomorrow morning. But you're going to probably have to stay home tomorrow and take care of the apartment."

Guy said, "You speak as if you have been through this before yourself."

Tess nodded. "Well, I have two kids. They go to school down the block." She pointed in the direction of PS 30.

"Must you go get them now?"

Tess shrugged. "They go to the free after-school program. It gives me a bit of time to get things done upstairs before I pick them up."

Guy nodded slowly, his eyes sweeping over the naked fingers of her left hand. "I don't suppose you could give me some help with this? Show me what to buy?"

Tess hesitated, her eyes darting around, wondering what any remaining parents would think if they saw them walking out together. But the school yard was mostly vacant now. She bit her lip.

"Just let me run upstairs and get my things. I'll meet you outside the gate."

CHAPTER 8

The aisles of the brightly lit pharmacy were narrow and crammed with merchandise all claiming to do the same thing. Tess let her eyes sweep the shelves, feeling Guy's helpless and agitated gaze on her, until she found the familiar white-and-red bottles.

"Here it is," she proclaimed, and handed it to him.

He smiled in gratitude and squinted at the instructions, his face contorted with effort as he tried to understand.

Tess bit her lip and then explained: "You just have to shampoo it in, leave it for ten minutes, and then rinse." She paused before continuing. "If I were you I'd do it in the morning before school, too. If they're in the apartment, they'll just go back in his hair while he's sleeping. Then he'll be sent home."

She picked up a second bottle and handed it to him. "This is for after. Put it on every day. It's to help keep new eggs from forming and to make the hair slippery so it's easier to use the comb."

She glanced at Yves, who was crouched over the bottom shelf, examining bottles of sugary kids' vitamins with cartoon characters on them.

Tess hesitated for a moment before suggesting, "Um, I don't suppose he'd want to cut his hair?"

In truth, Tess thought he ought to do this anyway. She didn't think Guy understood that it wasn't quite the style in America for boys to wear ponytails.

But Guy shook his head and opened his eyes wide. "Oh no, he won't. He's very stuck with his ponytail."

Tess laughed. "Well, we better go find the nit comb. This way!" She crooked a finger and headed to the hairbrush and comb area.

Outside, the sun angled carroty light onto the front of the building, reflecting off the glass and onto the sidewalk. The squeals of children from the overcrowded playground across the road competed with the traffic sounds of Smith Street, and streams of parents carrying children's school bags bustled after their careening, scooter propelled progeny. They, in turn, were oblivious to the fashionably tousled hipsters who angled out of their way.

And yet there was a feeling of quiet peacefulness in the air, like an idyllic New York moment one saw at the beginning of films as the camera swooped in from above.

"Well," Tess said, "I hate to break it to you, but Yves's hair is just the beginning. You're going to have to go through everything in the apartment and wash it…Do you have a washing machine?"

Tess's building had a shared laundry room, but she was aware that most of her friends had to haul bags to the laundry mat: one of the joys of New York City living.

Guy said, "It's a house, and they have it, yes."

Tess looked at him, surprised. "You rented a house?" It seemed a bit extravagant for just a single father and his son.

Guy shook his head. "It is, what do you call—a sublease? I am here working for a company who makes computer games. It is for one year only. This house belongs to a professor who is also gone away to work for one year only, so I rent it from him."

A tiny stone dropped into Tess's stomach, and she realized she had been lying to herself about how attracted she was to Guy.

"Stop it," she chastised herself. "Ain't gonna happen."

She smiled bravely. "Great! Well, good luck!"

She reached out to shake his hand, but he locked eyes with her and took her hand only after a significant pause. Then he traced his thumb briefly and lightly across the back of her wrist, delivering molten heat throughout her body. Sure that she was blushing, Tess glanced around to see if Yves was watching. But fortunately his back was turned, as he was poking dirt at the base of a tree with a stick.

"I will be too busy to shop tomorrow," Guy said. "Perhaps you will join me to eat somewhere?"

Tess tried to find her voice, but her throat had gone dry. When she was finally able, it came out as a croak—much to her embarrassment.

"I'm so sorry," she said. Her regret could not have been more genuine. "I can't go out with a parent. I'd lose my job."

Guy didn't say anything. He kept his eyes on hers, and Tess sensed that he was all too aware of their power. Something warm and slick worked its way up deviously from her stomach to the rest of her body. But she bit her lip and shook her head ruefully.

"I wish I could, but it would just be totally out of line."

Guy smiled with half his mouth and shook her hand loosely before releasing it. "I understand. I regret you cannot."

Tess looked down, frowning and trying to shake off the remorseful feelings. When she looked up again, she prayed that her eyes didn't betray her as she shrugged and put on a brave face. "I'll see you soon. Good luck with the…situation."

She swirled a finger and pointed it at Yves's head, smiling as she remembered his laughter. A look of nausea rose in Guy's eyes, but he seemed to push the feeling aside quickly as he thanked her and bid her good-bye.

Tess walked away, feeling somewhat sick with regret, imagining how some other single mom, one with a good handle on fashion and flirting, would snap Guy up in no time. Tess knew she was attractive to men, but she also knew men didn't like to work too hard to get what they wanted, and she wasn't fooling herself. Guy was just in New York for a short time. He wasn't looking to be any body's boyfriend.

CHAPTER 9

The lights had just dimmed when a bearded waiter deposited a lit beaker of a candle on the low, round table Tess and Molly sat in front of, ensconced in a floral-patterned couch reminiscent of the Brady Bunch.

"Did you get that from the religious-items store down the street?" Molly asked him teasingly.

The store was a neighborhood eyesore, with dusty shelves of comically clichéd religious symbols: merry green Buddhas and lenticular renderings of Jesus on the cross, which either stared at you or let you pass with disregarding eyes.

The waiter smiled and nodded. "Either for praying or for ambiance, depending on your point of view, I guess."

Molly made friends wherever she went, Tess reflected. Unlike Tess, she could initiate conversations with just about anyone—about their cute babies or whatever middle school they were gossiping about. Tess wished she had just a tenth of Molly's social confidence, which extended to men, and for a reason. Molly was hot, and she radiated cool. She was half Thai, and her face was an adorable mixture of freckles, sparkling dark eyes, and a row of perfectly straight, white teeth.

But despite her popularity, she had chosen Tess to be a close friend and confidante. In that way she was like Courtney. They were similar in many others ways too, she reflected, including the genuine way they were interested in hearing the details of other people's lives and problems, and always knew the perfect thing to say to make them feel better.

Now, sitting with her back to the ironically tacky gas fireplace, decorated for Halloween with dripping orange candles and skeleton heads on the mantle, she regarded Tess with reassuring sincerity.

"I don't know if what you're saying is true though, Tess," she said. "I mean, about Patrick never loving you. I think he must have at one time. He had to."

Tess bit her lip and shook her head. It was sweet of Molly to try and put a positive spin on her divorce, but she knew they were different in that way. Molly couldn't absorb that some people were just bad, or deviant, and there was no good side to appeal to. Tess preferred the truth. No matter how painful, the truth was more important to her than anything, and telling herself comforting lies did not make her feel better.

That's what she had had in mind when, after discovering everything about Patrick's running around on her, she had appealed to him, "Did you ever love me?"

But he had just shrugged. "I don't know. All I know is that, at this point, I don't. I don't love you, and I don't care about you or what happens to you."

She had been stunned into silence, but she knew the words were true. She had unmasked him. He had no need to pretend anymore, and he was probably pretty damn tired of doing so. When he spoke, his voice was stripped of a pretense that she had never before understood coated every word he'd ever said to her.

Now she looked at Molly. "I know it's hard to believe, but no, he didn't. That's sociopaths. They don't ever experience romantic love. It drives them crazy that other people do, so they turn to sex addiction, deception, and using the other person's love to manipulate and—I don't know—*minimize* them to make themselves feel better. To win, somehow…"

Tess searched for the right phrase, but she couldn't come up with the words to explain what Patrick had done to her. What had her cousin Will said after the divorce—when Tess had come to Toronto for a visit on

Christmas, all alone because Patrick had the children? "During the marriage, it was like I didn't recognize you."

And it was true, she knew. She had put whole chunks of her personality on the shelf to please Patrick. Slowly, she was reclaiming those lost bits. Now she smiled and looked at her friend, who was taking a swig from her beer and looking into the ornately framed mirror that hung above their heads on the wall opposite. In it, Tess could see that the restaurant was filling up with carefully tousled hipsters, though fortunately most of the newcomers were congregating around the bar, and their end was still pretty quiet.

Molly swallowed. "I know it's a really painful process...but look at me and Harold. I mean, we can be in the same room together now. We can even stand and joke together. I love that about us."

Tess shook her head. "But Molly, Harold *apologized*. He didn't stop apologizing. He felt *guilty* for running off with another woman and leaving you with the boys. If I could just get that—a simple apology—maybe things could move in that direction."

Molly gave her arm a brief squeeze. "Well, maybe you will. One day."

Tess let it drop. She knew she wouldn't. Patrick didn't experience remorse. It wasn't part of his hardware. As inconceivable as that was to most people, Tess knew it to be true. Patrick thought himself to be above the rules, above everyone and everything. He didn't, in his opinion, owe Tess a thing.

She shook off the bad feeling and asked brightly, "So how's it going with Bill? I saw your vacation pictures on Facebook. It looked amazing."

Molly smiled, and her eyes dazzled. Tess was glad to see her so happy. "It was amazing. Bill took care of everything—the resort, flights—he was so sweet. I wouldn't necessarily recommend just going to the D. R. for a vacation—the town looked pretty seedy—but the resort was really beautiful."

Tess sighed. "You're so fucking lucky. And, of course, you got to have sex, right? What's that like again?"

Molly laughed and then became a little melancholy. "You know, to be honest, he makes me feel like a sex fiend or something sometimes."

Tess looked at her, confused.

Molly explained. "I always have to initiate. Just once in a while, I'd like him to lose control and throw me down on the bed."

Tess took in Molly's flawless figure. "I can't believe he *doesn't!*"

"No," Molly said. "I think he smokes too much pot. It's like he's in a rut or something."

Tess tilted her head, wondering at Molly's reasoning. Surely Bill wouldn't have been able to bring pot onto an airplane and through customs in The Dominican Republic? And anyway, Bill was a lawyer. He would never be so stupid as to take a chance like that, surely?

She said, "Well, I sure as hell miss it. I'd happily throw a man down on the bed. That is, if I could agree to get one to be in the same room with me. Honestly! I'm on all those dating sites and I get nothing—nothing but losers and perverts. It's like, put a four in front of your age, and you might as well say you have AIDS."

Molly retorted, "You're only forty-two. And you look great, Tess. You know that."

The door gusted open, and Tess glanced up at the mirror as she took a sip from her beer. She nearly choked on it when she saw Guy saunter in, his arm draped over the shoulders of a single mother from her class, who was, Tess had to admit, one of the hottest moms in the hood.

Molly said, "Are you okay?" just as Tess slid down on the sofa to hide.

"I'm okay," Tess said, although she was sure her panicked expression betrayed her. "It's just that two single parents from my class—apparently on a date—just walked in."

Molly didn't swivel. Casually, she put her hand under her hair and adjusted it over the other shoulder, then turned her head. Then she spun back and hunkered down to Tess's level.

"Holy fuck, he's gorgeous!" she said, and laughed.

Tess couldn't help it—she began to giggle.

"Jesus, Tess, but don't get so freaked out, okay? I mean, I know they're parents and everything, but so are you."

Tess kept her mouth shut about her crush on Guy—and how he had asked her out and she had refused. Suddenly, it seemed like an imperative to just get out of there. "I just feel weird. I mean, what if they kiss or something?"

Molly shrugged. Tess knew she didn't understand the subtleties involved with being a teacher in the neighborhood where one lived. "Do you want to leave?"

Tess nodded. She fished some money out of her jeans pocket and deposited it on the table. Molly opened her purse and did the same.

"That's more than enough," Tess said. "We just had a couple of beers." She snuck a look behind her shoulder. Guy and the mother, whose name was Gina, were seated at the corner table behind the glass door. If Molly went first, Tess could scoot out behind her without being seen. She told her friend of her plan.

The music boomed one of Tess's favorite songs: "Three Pistols" by the Tragically Hip. She focused on it, keeping her head down as they slipped out.

Once outside, Molly laughed and looked at her. "Honestly, Tess, you should have just said hi!"

Tess looked back toward the bar. Through the glass she could see that Guy was leaning in toward his date. His mouth brushed hers and then moved in for a more purposeful kiss, as he let a strand of Gina's dark, wavy hair curl around his index finger. Tess felt simultaneously sick and turned on.

When she looked back, there was a knowing look on Molly's face, and her arms were folded across her unbuttoned shearling coat.

"Oh, I see how it is."

Tess flushed, then smiled weakly.

Molly punched her arm. "Honestly, Tess, just go for it, okay? Gina's a fucking idiot. He's not with her for her personality, and you know it. If you think there's a chance…"

But Tess shook her head. "I can't jeopardize my job, Moll. Not if I want to buy Patrick out of the apartment, and then I'll have to make mortgage payments. There's too much on the line."

She sighed and glanced back at the couple, now chatting. "Anyway, he's only here for the year."

Molly rolled her eyes. "Yeah, I wasn't actually thinking wedding bells. I just want you to have some fun. You deserve it."

And Tess looked at her and silently agreed.

CHAPTER 10

The white candlesticks in their silver holders cast buttery halos on the linen tablecloth, sprinkled with bread crumbs from the traditional *challah* bread and dotted with grape juice. Outside, swirls of purple October twilight tugged in the dark, and the swish and rustle of wind upsetting trees could be heard through the cracked window in the living room. Crooning softly in the background, the medley of Sabbath tunes were a nostalgic reminder of Tess's childhood and of the elaborate Sabbath dinners her mother used to prepare. Then, grandparents, cousins, aunts and uncles would gather around the table, made extra-long with a card table where she and her younger cousins would sit. Between courses they got up to let an uncle catch their nose, or to construct a wobbly castle from colored blocks, to be manned by dolls who mostly had no hair—thanks to Tess—but who were still required to fulfill the role of either prince or princess.

Her mother made everything from scratch: matzo ball soup, roast chicken or baked brisket with onions so soft that they melted in Tess's mouth. She remembered her favorite dishes: potato kugel and *tsmis*, a sweet cinnamon-and-honey-bathed mixture of carrots, sweet potatoes, and prunes. Even the challah was homemade, and desserts were cakes and pies that her mother and great-grandmother devoted one Friday a month to preparing, then stored in the giant freezer downstairs. The smell of the house on those Fridays wafted warm and welcoming down the street, and her cousins, on their way home from the nearby middle school, would always find an excuse to stop by for a cheese Danish or a piece of

Mandelbrot with a glass of milk. Tess also remembered *Zmiros*—songs— that everyone would sing together after dinner, with a sincerity that lifted her spirits.

In contrast, her children ate store-bought rotisserie chicken and roasted potatoes or rice. Dessert was brownies from a mix or a slice of Greene's chocolate babka with sugared strawberries. In truth, Tess had to push herself to pass along her Jewish background to her children. She never really wanted to make Shabbat or prepare for the holidays, but she forced herself anyway. From some corner of her mind, she knew without understanding why, that it was important. But she also knew that this compulsion came from her mind and not her heart. Anyway, her children looked forward to her Sabbath meals and were always disappointed if, for some reason, they couldn't have them. Tess was glad to have achieved at least that.

Now she regarded her children lovingly but bit back her admonishments for their abysmal table manners. When had she learned to put her napkin on her lap without thinking or not to eat with her fingers? Why couldn't she manage to instill this basic level of manners in her own children? Probably because she was a pushover. Probably because they knew she'd never do anything really bad to punish them, she thought.

Not that her own parents had been so strict. They were "of a type," Tess reflected: Her mother was a homemaker active in the community, and her father had a well-established dental practice in the strip mall across from her school, where almost everyone she knew went to get their teeth cared for. Sometimes when Tess was young, if he didn't have a patient scheduled, he would pick Tess up from school. Tess always felt so proud of him in his white dentist's smock, as they walked hand in hand across the street to the Big Scoop ice cream parlor. There she would order either a scoop of pink bubble-gum ice cream with real gumballs on a sugar cone, or a basket of French fries doused in white vinegar and salt. Any arguments or conflicts Tess might have had with her classmates during the day were forgotten when they met there, and their parents, who had also grown up together, chatted amicably like old friends.

Then her mother would arrive and take her, and her father would return to work for an hour or two. Sometimes they went to the Safeway before getting in the car. Tess could still remember the waft of baking smells that greeted her when she entered the supermarket. Dressed in her uniform of a pleated navy-blue tunic and white blouse, she had felt her difference from the public-school children who entered alongside their parents. She had reminded herself that, even though she wanted to pick up one of those yellow cupcakes with piles of pastel frosting and cram it into her mouth, it was probably made with lard, which wasn't kosher.

She laughed at this now. When was the last time she ate anything kosher anyway? Probably at her own kids' Hebrew school events, she thought ruefully.

She smiled and addressed her son, who chewed on a mouthful of roast chicken smothered in ketchup. "And what was the best thing that happened to you this week?"

Sammy knitted his brows and pressed his knuckles into his cheeks, still chewing. After an audible swallow, he said, "Reading bunnies. I have a new reading bunny. I forget her name, but she's really nice."

Rosie burst into giggles, and Sammy scowled and threw a fistful of rice at her. Rosie started to cry.

"He's so mean!" Rosie cried, as grains of rice tumbled out of her long brown hair. She brushed still more off her blue-striped shirt onto the floor.

Tess groaned inwardly. When would she learn? Just let them eat in silence. Trying to converse always led to arguments. "Sammy, don't you ever, ever throw food! Use your words if you're angry."

Sammy was indignant. "She was laughing at me!"

Rosie protested, "That's because you said reading *bunnies*. It's reading *buddies*."

"You don't know everything."

Tess employed her top-notch parenting skills. "Okay, everybody, just stop talking. Sammy, don't react with violence. Rosie, don't laugh at your brother."

"But I couldn't help it! It was funny!"

She looked at her daughter seriously. "Yes, you could help it."

The phone rang. Thank God. Tess went into the kitchen to answer it, tension a tightening cord hooked between her shoulder blades.

"It's your mother."

Tess sighed. Since her divorce, Tess's mother had always started the conversation with the same aggrieved sentence. It all began when Patrick refused to leave the apartment, dating women from online hookup sites, or just regular hookers, and then threatening Tess with violence, screaming in her face if she told him she would bolt the door. She shivered, remembering how his lawyer had threatened to have the police break down the door when he had gone out on a date on her birthday—not caring that their children would see and be traumatized.

But Rachel Shapiro had tried. She'd gotten on an airplane. She'd flown to New York. She'd said to Patrick, "You are *not* allowed to treat my daughter this way, do you understand?"

And Patrick had sat there, his arms folded over his pot belly, glowering at her. "Oh, I understand. I just disagree."

Her mother had flown into a rage at that point, screeching at him to "just get out," which Tess understood and appreciated. The only problem was that the whole drama played out in front of her children, the one thing Tess had promised herself she would never let happen. No matter what, her children were not to know what their father did. But in one fell swoop, her mother had shattered that protective bubble, and Tess was angrier at her than she deserved.

For the first time in her life, she yelled at her mother. Actually she yelled at her mother to "shut the fuck up," which had done wonders for their already fractured relationship. Since then, despite Tess's attempts at reconciliation, her mother still held a grudge.

"How are you?" Her mother sniffed.

Tess tried to inject warmth into her voice. "I'm good. Tired but okay. How are you?"

To her horror, her mother began to sob. "No one invites me anywhere!"

Tess groaned sympathetically. "Oh, Mom! I wish you'd just move back to Vancouver! Your whole family is there."

Her mother blew her nose audibly.

"You know that's not true. Your aunt and uncle are here, and their children. And…there's other reasons why I won't go back there. You wouldn't understand."

Tess pressed her lips together and chewed them, staring at her reflection in the darkened kitchen window. She thought she did understand. Her mother had moved east out of embarrassment. After her father had died, Tess's mother had had a string of torrid affairs with men, none of whom were Jewish, and all of whom were rich. Then there was the spending—all the new clothes and flamboyant hairstyles, the renovations to the house… People had talked, and Rachel Shapiro, once a revered pillar of her community, had been obviously shunned.

Tess felt sorry for her mother, living in an apartment by herself in downtown Toronto. She shopped to make herself feel better and worked in real estate to make money to shop more. Tess knew the day was coming when the money would run out and then it would all come crashing down on her head—and on Tess's.

"I just wondered if you saw the news," her mother said. "Some big bank in Paris was bombed. Mondiale? Something like that. It was that terrorist group they've been talking about, NAFKA?"

Tess knitted her brows. "Oh my God, when did this happen? I didn't hear."

Her mother's voice assumed its "juicy gossip with relish" tone. Tess knew she loved to be the first one to break whatever pending newsflash was being reported. "Well, it was just a few hours ago, I think. I hadn't lit the candles yet."

Tess felt a pang of pity, thinking of her mother lighting the Sabbath candles alone. They had never been a terribly observant family. They kept the house kosher so anyone they knew could come eat there, but they didn't keep the traditional rules of Sabbath and in general ate at whatever restaurant they felt like. So Tess was surprised when her mother clung to this observance every Friday night, even though she lived by herself now, and wondered if it didn't make her even more depressed.

Tess walked over to the computer, glancing at her children, who were finishing their supper. She covered the mouthpiece. "If you're done, you can watch a little TV before dessert. Just keep it down. I'm on the phone."

They got up in unison, excited, Tess knew, to see what Friday-night Disney movie was on.

Tess turned on the computer screen and went to CNN. Sure enough, images of another smoldering building were front and center. She clicked through the slide show of bodies being dragged out, of ash and fire inter-mixing with heaps of concrete stones, of jagged lengths of singed steel cables piercing the smoke-filled sky.

"Jesus."

"I know," her other intoned. "Are you looking at the pictures now?"

Tess gulped and nodded. "It looks like the Towers after 9/11."

"That's just what I was thinking!"

"It's amazing," Tess said and huffed. "The world is going crazy. Radical Islamic terrorists were bad enough, but now this! And I don't even under-stand what they want or who they are!"

"They're German, of course," her mother said matter-of-factly. "They just can't stand that France is gaining the upper hand in Europe. You know Germans. It was the same before the wars. They think the world should recognize that they're naturally superior."

Tess felt repelled. "Mom, it's not *Germany*. It's just a small group of radicals inside Germany. You can't blame the whole country."

Her mother sounded indignant. "Yes, I can. If the German government wanted to get rid of those horrible people, they could. It was the same with Hitler. They just turned a blind eye, and look what happened!"

Tess didn't know what to say to that, so she changed the subject. "Do you want to say hello to the children?"

"Of course I do!"

Tess went into the kitchen to start cleaning up as Rosie and Sammy took turns telling Rachel about school and weekend plans and what they were going to dress up as for Halloween. At the mention of Halloween, Tess felt a sickening lurch, remembering last Halloween—how Patrick had insisted on coming but had spent the whole time scrolling through his harem on OkCupid and smiling to himself as he texted.

Then she heard Rosie's voice begging, "Can't you come, Grandma? Please? You can sleep in my room," followed by a chorus of "Yays!" that made her freeze midtask.

Rosie marched into the kitchen, pointing the phone at Tess like a pistol.

"Grandma says she can come and stay with us for Halloween and come trick-or-treating. She wants to talk to you first, though."

Tess took a deep breath and dried her hands on her apron. "Hey, Mom."

"The children want me to come for Halloween, but I didn't want to say yes until I made sure it was all right with you. I don't want to be a burden." She spoke with an affected stoicism that made Tess look up at the ceiling.

"Of course I want you to come," she said automatically.

She could almost hear her mother's gratified smile. "Well, that's wonderful. I'll e-mail you the dates after I buy my ticket."

Tess nodded and bit her lip. "Okay, bye, Mom. Shabbat Shalom."

"Good Shabbos," her mother replied, using the old Yiddish Sabbath greeting, rather than the Hebrew one Tess and her generation had been taught in school.

CHAPTER 11

The children were asleep, and Tess was settled in her own bed, some drawing paper and a clipboard balanced on her knee as she chewed at a pencil absently, eyes staring at nothing. Beside her, a discarded calculator lay nestled in the sheets—for it was numbers, not anger, that now kept her from sleep.

The e-mail from the appraiser had come, and the estimate was higher than Tess had anticipated. Buying Patrick out of the apartment would mean taking out an additional loan—and not a little one either. She had done the math about ten times, and yes, she could make it—just—but she would be living in a state of financial insecurity for pretty much ever. If only there was a way she could make more money! If somehow she could just make an extra $1,000 per month, then she could make the extra loan and mortgage payments without stressing about bills.

Moving wasn't an option. Everything was here. The children's school, work, all their friends and hers...Besides, when would she find the time to find another place that would be suitable? And moving would be so time consuming and expensive, not to mention disruptive to every-one's lives.

Fucking Patrick! After all he had done, at least he could have the decency to just sign the mortgage over to her.

Stop trying to think of him in the context of what a normal person would do, she chided herself, but the anger welled up nonetheless, and her pencil carved deeply into the stack of crisp, white pages.

PANEL ONE

Andrea Chambers is sitting across the table from Anton and the small, dark-haired man. The room is sparse, but light shafts into the room from the windows behind the two men. A Swiss and an American flag stand next to each other in one corner to indicate that they are in the Swiss embassy.

A thought bubble extends from Andrea's head: "Sergeant Anton used to have a crush on me, I know he did. All those group punishments everyone had to do *au cause d'Andrea*...I always knew it was because he actually liked me. Now if only I could rekindle some of that old feeling, perhaps I could use it to my advantage."

PANEL TWO

Caption: "Fighter jets explode over the New York skies following a bomb attack at New York's Penn Station, killing 137 commuters in the most violent terror attack the city has seen since 9/11."

The panel depicts an aerial shot of New York City from just higher than the two fighter jets. Far below, we can see the the landmark buildings lining Thirty-Fourth Street: Macy's, Madison Square Garden, and Penn Station. A slew of emergency vehicles, small like toys from the great distance, are pulled up at irregular angles, their lights still flashing, their doors left open as if vacated in a moment of panic.

PANEL THREE

Anton leans across the table. "*Alors*, you want me to agree to let you and your children come to Switzerland now? And what will you do there? Why should we give you a visa? We have thousands of people applying at every moment."

PANEL FOUR

Andrea, dressed in a pencil skirt with high heels and an open-necked blouse, looks plaintive as she implores him to act in her favor. "I know you have so many applicants and every one of them feels as desperate as me. I just—I was hoping that, since I still have friends in the country, that because I went to school there and served in the army...I thought, perhaps—"

Anton snorts and rolls his eyes, tapping the eraser end of his pencil on the clipboard before him. "This was not the real army, and you went to a school for Canadians only! You have no more right to ask for this privilege than anyone."

PANELS FIVE THROUGH SIX

Andrea grips the armrests of her chair as Anton leans over to speak to the other man: *"Aller chercher l'arme et apportez-la ici."*

In a thought bubble, Andrea translates: "He's asking that man to bring a weapon of some sort. I wonder what for?"

The little dark man scurries out of the room and returns with a long package wrapped in brown paper, which he places on the table and unwraps.

Andrea gasps. "It's an M16, like we used in basic training!"

PANELS SEVEN THROUGH EIGHT

Anton nods. "Show me what you remember from basic training. Take the weapon apart and put it back together again."

Andrea focuses on the weapon as her hands move in a blur. In a thought bubble, she is trying to remember the process: "First, check that weapon is on safe, then the two side pins, yank open, coil, cylinders..."

She pauses and makes a big show of holding up the 'weekend' pin: "I remember that if we forgot to put this pin back in the gun, we'd lose our right to go home for the weekend!"

She finishes reassembly with a *clack!* and hands the weapon back to Anton, who shakes his head, refusing it.

PANEL TEN
Anton stands and beckons her to follow him into an adjacent room. "Bring this weapon with you," he commands.

PANEL ELEVEN
The second room is smaller than the first and has no windows. Andrea gasps when she sees Jonathan tied to a chair, no pillowcase over his face this time. He meets her gaze with steely anger and says, "What the fuck is going on? What am I doing here? What are *you* doing here?"

PANEL TWELVE
Anton hands Tess a brass-colored magazine for her machine gun. *"Tuer-le!"* ("Kill him!")

Andrea shakes her head. "Please, I can't kill my husband!"

PANELS THIRTEEN THROUGH FOURTEEN
Anton says, "If you do not kill him, no visa for you *or* your children. Either you show me you can be of some use to us, or you all three perish."

The words *Pound, Pound!* reverberate around Andrea's chest. Slowly, she pulls back the hammer, inserts the C-shaped magazine, and takes aim.

"Maintenenant!" Anton barks.

Andrea stands in position and looks through the viewfinder. Jonathan starts to scream, *"No-o-o!"* but the bullet reaches his neck, bursting it open and cutting off his final words.

It was after 2:00 a.m. when Tess awakened. Sammy was crawling soundlessly into her bed, clearly trying not to wake her, but a boom of thunder tugged her out of sleep at the same instant as he rested his head on the pillow beside her. Sammy always woke up during thunderstorms. They terrified him, and Tess had told him it was fine for him to come into her bed if he was scared, but just try not to wake her. Sadly, she was not a sound sleeper and his efforts rarely worked.

Hitching her head up to rest on the palm of one hand, her elbow on her pillow, she turned to look at him, his face so sweet and innocent in the darkened room. She slid one arm under his pajama top and rubbed his back until his breathing came deeper and she could tell he was as sound asleep as she was wide awake.

Sighing, she slipped out of bed and tiptoed out to the kitchen to get a glass of milk, grabbing her iPhone off the console in the hallway as she passed. As she sipped, standing next to the wooden carving board, she opened her Gmail again to look at the e-mail from the appraiser. There she saw there was an email from Patrick with the subject line MEETING.

Shit. He had probably heard about the appraisal and wanted to discuss figures and logistics. She had been hoping to have a few days to think things through before speaking to him. She winced and clicked on his message.

If you have some time this week, there's something I'd like to go over with you. Let me know when is a good time. Best, Patrick

Ugh. The last thing in the world she wanted was a face-to-face with him! It was so much easier to communicate with e-mails. But Patrick knew, she was sure, how uncomfortable she felt in his presence and no doubt got off on it. She gritted her teeth as she e-mailed him back.

After I drop the kids off at Hebrew school and before you pick them up makes the most sense. I'll meet you on Wednesday at 4:00 upstairs at Connecticut Muffin unless you e-mail me otherwise.

She didn't bother to sign her name. Really, she thought it was kind of weird that people signed their names on e-mail messages. I mean, it says right there who it's from. Why sign your name?

She took another swig of milk before carrying it and her phone over to the sofa. Outside, the sky crackled and boomed, and she cast a nervous glance toward her bedroom, hoping Sammy wouldn't wake up again. Fortunately, Rosie was a sound sleeper.

On impulse, she switched over to her work e-mail, thinking she'd probably be too groggy and out of it to remember to do so in the morning. Her heart leapt when she saw an e-mail message from Guy. She stared at it for several moments, holding some milk in her mouth, before clicking on the e-mail with her thumb and swallowing.

The subject was GOING AWAY, and the message read: *I'm sorry I didn't inform you earlier. You probably noticed Yves was not in school today.* (Tess hadn't. Yves's group had been in the French room that day.) *Unfortunately we must travel to Paris for one week for some family business. Yves will be out of school until October 17th.*

Tess's heart sped up, thinking of the Paris bombing. She e-mailed back: *I hope everyone is okay. I heard about the terrible bombing incident, and I hope it didn't impact your family in any way!*

She gasped in surprise when she received a reply just a few moments later: *No, but thank you for asking. They are all fine. It is actually for my nephew's Bar Mitzvah. I can't believe I forgot about it and had to book last-minute tickets. We left on Thursday after school.*

Tess mentally calculated that if he were already in France, it would be midmorning, which would explain how he was able to respond so quickly. She also noted with satisfaction that Guy didn't sign his e-mails.

She hesitated, biting her lip. *I didn't realize you were Jewish. Your last name is Noel! (I'm allowed to make comments like that because my last name is Shapiro.)*

She gritted her teeth and shut her eyes to obliterate the prickly feeling that tugged at her stomach lining—she didn't usually make such personal comments on emails to parents.

A moment later her phone buzzed again. *Yes, I am. Well, my mother was. It is a long story. I'll explain it when I take you to dinner next weekend.*

Tess laughed softly, reading the message again. Then she was quiet, focusing on the word *was* and wondering when and how Guy's mother had died. She was suddenly gripped by a painful yearning for her own father, someone strong and stable who would have been there for her, to protect her and guide her through all the pain of the past year.

A rush of rain echoed off the sidewalk and hoods of cars and pinged on the air-conditioning units. Sammy moaned in his sleep, and Tess got up to return to him.

CHAPTER 12

Tess pulled her battered red Honda Accord up to the curb in front of the synagogue on Remsen Street, and the children tumbled out, racing each other up the stairs.

"See you tomorrow!" she called after them. "Have fun at Daddy's!"

They waved and smiled, greeting the laughing security guard with high-fives as they entered. Tess lingered a moment, watching them. She was glad they loved going to Hebrew school. If they didn't, she told them and herself on more than one occasion, they didn't have to go. She wasn't forcing them. But year after year they balked at the suggestion of not going, telling her they'd be really mad if she didn't sign them up again. And secretly, Tess was glad. She herself had grown up in a Jewish vacuum—not something she wanted for her own children—but she did want them to have a sense of where she came from.

Brooklyn Heights was a fairy tale of Victorian mansions, cobbled streets, arching maples, and charming cafés. Tess circled the streets idly, eyes peeled for a parking spot, then walked the three blocks back to Montague Street, the main thoroughfare in the affluent community. As she neared the muffin shop, her stomach clenched with nervousness. It had been almost a year since she'd had a conversation with Patrick that wasn't over e-mail or, if in front of the children, that wasn't fake and breezy.

She was halfway up the stairs to the second-floor sitting area at the coffee shop, small decaf in hand, when she caught sight of him. His face looked crumpled and sad; his eyes were cast down, ankles crossed and knees splayed out carelessly beneath the table. For a moment she froze, gripped by a wave of pity and a desire to hug him that immediately repulsed her. He still radiated a glow that had once been a source of attraction for her, but now she recognized this, from her psychologist's advice, as what was referred to as "the addict's glow." Stubbornly, she pushed the sympathetic impulse aside and continued up the stairs until she was standing in front of him.

He looked up then, but it took him a moment to recognize her. She sucked in her breath, realizing his expression of a moment before had had nothing to do with her. Possibly, he had been thinking about a failed relationship with another woman. With regards to Patrick's feelings about her, Tess told herself, her existence had been solely to fulfill the role of "person to cheat on." Really, he could have married a pineapple.

He nodded and said, "Hello," but did not smile.

Tess put her paper cup down on the table and sat down in front of him. The upstairs room was spacious but not crowded. Most of the tables were taken up by people sitting alone, nursing a coffee while tapping on their laptops. A row of windows overlooking Montague Street and the Heights bathed the space with gray, late-afternoon light. In one corner a pair of women gossiped avidly, their voices rising and falling like steam interrupted by sips from a searing cup of liquid.

Patrick said in an obligatory tone, "How are you?"

"I'm fine," she replied, just as robotically.

Patrick nodded. His expression didn't change. Then he lifted his eyes up to look at her; they were red and filled with pain. Again, she felt a spasm of pity that she fought to quell.

He said, "Well, I should come straight to the point. I have leukemia. I'm dying. I have about a year to live." He added as an afterthought, "I've just started chemo."

From downstairs, the sound of something breaking shattered the air. Tess did not blink. She stared at Patrick, unable to speak, as if it were he who had just raised a ceramic plate in the air and let it fall to the ground to smash to smithereens.

A glut of bile rose in her throat. How many times had she fantasized about his dying—often by her own hands—and now the news that it was actually happening left her wondering if the restroom was occupied, in case she needed to throw up.

She swallowed and shook her head, her eyes glued to his face. "I'm so sorry."

Patrick frowned and shrugged. His response felt like a slap. "I just wanted to talk to you about how to break it to the kids."

Tess looked at him; her face had gone slack. She doubted Patrick cared about the impact the news would have on the children's emotional world, but wondered at his true motives. It hadn't, she remembered, bothered him at all to tell the children about their divorce. Tess had been beside herself in anticipation of breaking the news, and had felt gutted afterward, but not him. In a chat between Patrick and a Facebook friend that Tess had seen, he said: *Sammy only cried because Tess cried.*

Yet it had been the other way around. Tess had cried when she saw Sammy burst into tears. Of course, Patrick couldn't see that. Not then and not now. He was simply not able.

Now all she could think about was how she couldn't sit down to another conversation like that, not even a year later. She imagined going through it again, with Patrick sitting there pretending to get—but not actually understanding—the emotional impact he was having on everyone, and she knew she couldn't do it. Suddenly she realized the real reason Patrick had summoned her to the meeting.

She said, "I'll tell them on a weekend when they're with me. Then I'll bring them to your place. They can spend the rest of the weekend there, and you can bring them to school on Monday."

He looked up at her with heavy lids. A mixture of surprise and gratitude filled his eyes. He was surprised that she would do him a favor. He didn't understand that, in fact, she was doing herself one.

She said, "It's better that way. I don't think we should tell them together as if we're still a family."

Her own words brought a sting of tears to her eyes. Thinking about her marriage and the dissolution of her family always caused this reaction. She knew she couldn't—not even for an hour—revisit that emotional no-man's-land upon which she had built a shadow of her former self.

Patrick nodded. Some color returned to his face, and he sat up straighter, picking pitifully at a carrot muffin that sat on its wrapper in front of him. The way he chewed and swallowed reminded her of a child eating after a tantrum. Pity welled up in her again, and she didn't try and stop it.

"I'll do it this weekend, if that works for you," she added.

Patrick nodded again and looked at her meaningfully. "Thank you. If you tell them on Saturday, you can bring them to me in the afternoon."

"Yes," Tess said. "Okay."

After several moments of silence, she got up to leave, but the swift action caused the room to lurch and spin. She gripped the back of the chair and took a deep breath.

Patrick's voice came automatically. "You okay?"

She nodded. He doesn't give a shit about you, she reminded herself, and the prompt helped her get a hold of herself. She swallowed, about to attempt the walk to the stairs, then remembered something.

"Patrick, about the apartment…does it matter now, about the buyout?"

He looked up at her, surprised. "Of course. I'm going to leave the money to my sister and her family."

Tess knew immediately that his justification to himself was that his sister and her family were poor, but it irked her nonetheless. He didn't care about her, and it hadn't occurred to him to put the money in trust for his own children—hadn't even *occurred* to him! She looked at him, nodded, and then walked out.

CHAPTER 13

October crept on like a stealthy ghost and, on the first Saturday after Patrick's announcement, the weather remained sunny and fairly warm. Tess wished she could just get the bikes out and take the kids for a ride down by the waterfront in neighboring Redhook. She loved these outings, when the weather turned just a little brisk, and the briny air put color into her children's cheeks. They always took the same route, cycling passed abandoned factories tattooed with colorful graffiti, and stopping to buy individual key lime pies at Steve's Pie Shop. These they ate on the elongated pier at the adjacent park, gazing out at the river, the Statue of Liberty, and the New Jersey shore.

Instead, she knew, it would be a terrible day—a day that would, once again, fracture the lives of her children into a before and after. And it was she, Tess, who was going to have to level that boom. She glowered at the sheaf of pages in front of her on her bedroom desk and breathed deeply. From the living room, sounds of Saturday-morning cartoons echoed inanely. The contrary pull of procrastination kept her fixed to her chair for a few stolen minutes as, guiltily, she began to draw.

PANEL ONE

Caption: "The Talmud Torah Elementary School in Lausanne Switzerland has been bombed by a group claiming to be affiliated with ISIS. Twenty-six students are still unaccounted for. The school bears the same name as the one Andrea attended as a child in Vancouver, Canada."

PANEL TWO

We see Andrea Chambers standing among the wreckage of the destroyed school, holding a handkerchief to her face. Tears stream down her cheeks as she surveys the scene of destruction.

The queue of volunteers lined up from the top of the pile to the bottom, passes bricks and jagged pieces of metal down the line. Andrea spots Jonathan at the top and a thought bubble proclaims, "Jonathan! What's he doing here?"

PANELS THREE THROUGH FOUR

A cheer comes up from the crowd: "HURRAY!"

Someone says: "They found someone and he's alive!"

The group at the top frantically pulls at pieces of sheet-rock, bars of wire, and chunks of bricks. Then Jonathan eases out a tiny body and lays him down gently on the pile of wreckage.

PANEL FIVE

A woman rushes forward from the crowd assembled below. "My son, my son!" she cries, as a team of medics swoop down on the young boy, who is unconscious.

PANEL SIX

The boy coughs and sputters, and Andrea doubles over with relief. A thought bubble says, "Thank goodness, he's going to be okay!"

PANEL SEVEN

Jonathan spots Andrea and makes his way down the mound toward her.

Andrea says, "Where are our children?"

Jonathan says, "They're at the hotel. They have a babysitting service there."

PANEL EIGHT
In the background, we see the boy on a stretcher, being eased onto an ambulance, followed by his mother.

Andrea looks at Jonathan. "What are you doing here?"

Jonathan shrugs. "I'm helping."

PANEL NINE
Behind Tess, a taxi cab waits with its door open. The driver looks at Andrea expectantly.

She says, "I...I have to go back. I have to get back to work. The children have to get back to school. I'm going back to the hotel and get them, and then we have to go to the airport."

Jonathan says, "Okay. I guess I'll stay here for a while. They need all the help they can get."

PANEL TEN
Andrea looks at him in amazement. "But what about *your* work? And anyway, aren't there enough volunteers here in Switzerland?"

Jonathan shrugs and looks off into the distance. "To be honest, Andrea, from what I'm hearing, people don't give too much of a shit about the Jews around here."

PANEL ELEVEN

Andrea looks angry. "Maybe you just like playing the hero. Makes you feel better about yourself?"

Jonathan looks down. "Maybe. It does feel good to help people. Anyway, I think I'll stay on."

PANEL TWELVE

Andrea grimaces. "Suit yourself. Nice to see you giving such a shit about other people's families, by the way! Too bad you never were able to care about your own."

Jonathan looks at her. "I really don't need your insights into my motives, Andrea. Thanks anyway, though."

PANEL THIRTEEN

Andrea sits in the backseat of the taxi cab, watching Jonathan ascend the heap of debris once again. There are tears in her eyes.

Jonathan says to no one in particular, "When is that canine unit supposed to get here, anyway?"

Tess regarded her work and huffed. She was still angry at Patrick, despite his illness, for not relenting on the buyout. Now, she stared out her bedroom window, where gusts of leaves floated between her building and the one next door.

As she went to put her latest installment in her chest, it occurred to her—not for the first time—that maybe there was a way to make money off her comic-book habit. In truth, she had always wanted Patrick to see her comics and had on a several occasions offered—actually asked—to show him, but he wouldn't look for some reason. He always brushed her off so that finally she stopped asking. Instead, she left the chest unlocked in her room, imagining that one day he would take the initiative and look inside it himself. Then, she thought, he would come out of their room and put his arms around her and tell her what a genius she was.

But he never did, so she came to think possibly he had, in fact, looked at them and thought they were bad or stupid and something embarrassing that she really ought to keep to herself.

Her chest squeezed and her stomach clenched in anxious anticipation. Sounds of *Sponge Bob Square Pants* yammering in the living room drifted to her ears, and Tess squeezed her eyes shut for a final moment before heading there.

Her children lay on the couch in their pajamas like they did every Saturday morning. Their eyes—if she were to draw them in comic-book form—would have hypnotic swirls instead of irises, as they stared at the wall-mounted television. Cushions had been kicked carelessly onto the floor, and legs hung across the backside of the sectional where they sprawled, a portrait of lethargy.

They hardly noticed when Tess took a seat between them, but moaned in protest when she informed them that the TV had to go off after the episode they were watching.

"You've been watching for two hours!" she reminded them.

"Okay," Sammy relented. Rosie was silent.

The ordeal of turning off the set always included recording the next show, and Tess waited patiently, in no hurry to get on with the task at hand.

Sammy stretched and rested his head on her lap. "So what are we going to do today?"

He closed his eyes like a contented kitten as she stroked his hair. Rosie looked out the window and traced her finger briefly on the glass. Tess didn't bother to admonish her for leaving prints.

As if reading Tess's earlier thoughts, Rosie said, "Can we ride our bikes?"

Tess offered a weak smile. "Maybe," she croaked.

Rosie looked at her, and her expression turned inquisitive. "Mom, are you okay?"

Sammy turned his head and peered up at her. Tess had to unglue her tongue from the roof of her mouth before she could speak. "I'm afraid I have some bad news."

Rosie's eyes widened. "How bad, Mom? What's wrong?"

Tess held out her arm for Rosie to come in close. She dove into the spot and pulled Tess's arm across her own shoulder. Tess looked down at her and Sammy.

"It's about Daddy."

And she told them, in as gentle a voice as possible, what Patrick had told her. They stared up at her in stunned silence, tears streaming down their cheeks. Tears pricked at Tess's own eyes, but she forced them back. She must, she told herself, be strong for the children.

Sammy began to howl, and Tess gathered him in her arms and kissed the top of his head.

Rosie said, "When is Daddy going to die, Mommy?"

This made Sammy howl louder, and Tess squeezed him tight, rocking him like a much younger child. "Baby, I don't know. He's getting lots of special medicine."

Then she remembered what she'd learned in teacher's college: *What children imagine is always worse than the truth. It's best to be honest.*

She took a deep breath. "He probably will live another year. That's what he told me anyway."

Rosie looked away, silent tears still streaming down her cheeks. The sun from the window cast half of Rosie's face in light, and Tess felt as though she were discovering a new side of her. She was a person of great insight and dignity, despite her young years.

Tess was taken with the recollection of the morning when she'd woken up and found out about Patrick. She had gotten up early as usual to sip her coffee in peace. Halfway through drinking it, she went over to check the weather and her e-mail on the computer. When the screen came to life, there was a chat between Patrick and another woman. It was the rows of heart emoticons that first caught her eye. Then she began to read: They loved each other. He did not love Tess. Tess was crazy, obsessive—a shrill, irrational hysteric. Her Patrick! He said these things! About her! And the tone of it—not the Patrick she knew. This someone was suave, witty, and apparently unconsciously adorable. She had never met this person.

How the hell had she got through that morning? But she had. She'd made her children breakfast, packed their lunches, put their schoolbags in order, and taken them to school.

She did this every day, but on that morning, in some intuitive compassion, Rosie had said, "Hey, Mom, thanks for packing my stuff for me."

Tess had turned, blinking back tears, and said "Oh, you're welcome! And thank you for saying thank you!"

Sammy now interrupted her reverie. Sniffling, but in a firm voice, he said, "I want to see Daddy now."

Tess nodded. "Yes," she said. "I thought that would be a good idea. Why don't you guys get dressed, and I'll drive you over there?"

Rosie looked at her. "But, Mom, this is supposed to be our weekend with you."

Tess stroked her hair. "This is a special circumstance, sweetie. We're going to make an exception. Daddy wants to see you, and I think you should see him."

Rosie nodded and got up to blow her nose on a paper towel in the kitchen.

Sammy said, "I'm going to go get dressed now."

He stomped off to his room.

"Okay," Tess said. "I'll text Daddy that we'll be there in twenty minutes."

From her spot in front of the fire hydrant, Tess waited in the car and watched as Patrick opened the door of his building to let the children in. After the door closed behind them, she stared, blinking, for several minutes. Then she lowered her forehead onto the steering wheel and let the pent-up emotion of the morning come out in giant, spasmodic sobs.

CHAPTER 14

By evening, Tess was feeling significantly better. She had spent lunch with Molly, eating smoked-meat sandwiches at the Eighth Street Deli and discussing Tess's situation. Molly did her best to convince her that the reason she felt sad was because Patrick had loved her once, and she had loved him, and he was the father of her children, and they loved him. Tess wasn't sure, but just being in Molly's company always cheered her up, and by the end she felt more like herself—and more ready for her date that evening with Guy.

Molly nearly choked when Tess told her. "I thought you said you'd never!"

Tess laughed. "You were the one who told me to go for it!"

Molly nodded, her lips pressed in a satisfied smile. "Good," she said. "You need this, Tess."

"No one can find out," Tess said severely.

Molly brought her hand to her chest. "They won't hear it from me."

Broadway smelled like it always did this time of year, Tess reflected as she made her way out of the subway station—like roasted peanuts and wet bark. The street had the air of a fairground that had just been closed for the night. Overflowing rubbish bins were expended, dormant volcanoes at every corner.

Few people strolled up the commercial avenue now, though she knew that just hours before it had been thronged with shoppers and tourists.

Behind the glass of the brightly illuminated stores, wilting sales clerks used their last shreds of energy to tidy up, returning merchandise to hangers and folding tumbles of sweaters into neat piles on tables.

In Soho, the atmosphere changed to one of quiet sophistication. Home to exclusive clothing boutiques, high-end furniture stores, and irreproachably cool restaurants, the deserted fair ground atmosphere seemed far from its cobbled streets. Here, small clutches of stylishly attired people ambled to destination restaurants and bars, as the trill of laughter echoed off the polished stone buildings. Tess regarded them enviously, imagining their lives filled with evenings like these. She ran her fingers through her hair self-consciously until it felt smooth and bounced on her shoulders as she walked. This she did carefully, as she was unused to wearing the high-heeled leather boots that her mother had insisted on buying her at Henry Bendel's on her last visit.

Guy was already waiting outside the restaurant, looking even more dazzling than usual in an expensive pair of jeans, gray buttoned shirt, and black leather jacket. Tess caught her breath when she saw him leaning against the wall near the entrance-way, his head cocked slightly to one side, obviously watching her approach before she spotted him. The twinkling, amused smile was there again, and she squinted and looked at him sideways as she approached.

"What's so funny?"

Guy just laughed and kissed her on the forehead, and Tess smiled so as not to betray her melting insides.

The restaurant was crowded with young, attractive people. Smells of butter and garlic permeated the air, and a glowing fireplace crackled at the base of a stone wall opposite the door. Tess was glad to be seated at a quiet table in a corner, where she wouldn't have to strain to hear Guy above the other patrons.

When a good-looking waitress in a miniskirt, who somehow recognized a fellow ex-patriot, flirted with Guy in French as she handed them menus, Tess struggled to keep her expression indifferent. But one look at Tess's face after the waitress had departed caused Guy to burst into laughter.

Tess's cheeks flamed, and she felt a hot lick of anger. Guy smothered his outburst and patted her hand. In a calm and serious voice he said, "Tess, please. I'm flattered." She relaxed and he added, "And I couldn't be more happy that you agreed to meet me here tonight."

His eyes were soft and sincere. Tess conceded a half smile.

Since it was a French restaurant anyway, and to cover her ignorance about the topic, she let Guy choose the wine, and used the time to ponder the menu. Too late, she remembered that she wasn't really a fan of French high cuisine. It had just been so long that she'd forgotten how everything was covered in so much sauce. But the wine, when it came, was sweet and delicious.

Guy raised his glass. "To beginnings," he said.

She flushed, greeting his toast with a clink of her own glass and wishing she were brave enough to say something so forward.

He said, "You look beautiful, by the way."

Tess felt herself blush again. "Thank you," she said, and released a shuddering breath. She hated how she never knew how to take a compliment.

When the waitress returned, Tess took the safe bet and ordered steak frites. Guy had a fish dish that, when it arrived, made her glad she had erred on the side of unexciting. It had so much white sauce on it that it reminded her of a dissolving Eskimo pie.

Guy seemed to enjoy it however, even offering her a bite, which she refused. They spoke of their children, and Tess was pleased to note that Guy was not the sort of parent who bragged about his child, although he most certainly could have done. Yves was very bright.

She gave as few details as possible about her divorce; Guy might imagine she had caught some disease from all of Patrick's philandering. She remembered how afraid she had been of this herself; how she had taken a panicked trip to a midtown clinic. Fortunately, everything had come out normal.

"He had other women," she explained simply. "And when I found out, he just said he didn't want to be married anymore."

She didn't mention Patrick's illness. She didn't want to think about that now. Every time she remembered, a bitter stream of bile raced up her throat, burning her tonsils before retreating sourly into her stomach. She took a gulp of water, hoping Guy wouldn't notice her emotional battle.

But he regarded her with eyes full of sympathy, his fork poised halfway between his plate and chin. A little white chunk of fish plopped onto the pile of sauce with a splatter.

He said, "A woman like you is not for a man like this. It is a crime, what he did."

Tess stared at him. No one had ever spoken to her like that. "Really, it wouldn't have mattered who he was married to. He just got off on cheating."

She thought of the way her cousin Will put it: "That's his bingo."

But Guy shook his head. "Men who are like this, they marry other sorts. It is criminal that he did this to you."

Tess bit her lip. Feeling uncomfortable and unsure of how to respond, she changed the subject. "So you were at a Bar Mitzvah, you said? In Paris?"

Guy took a sip of wine and held it in his mouth a moment before swallowing. "Yes. My mother, you see, she was Jewish, but my father was not. This was for my nephew—well, cousin really, but we were raised as brothers—on my mother's side."

Tess's mouth fell slightly open as she pieced together what he had said. "Your parents passed away? Both of them? And your cousin—you were raised by your aunt and uncle?"

Guy nodded and set his glass down. "Yes, a long time ago. My sister was nine, and I was eleven when my parents were killed in an automobile accident. We were sent to live with this aunt—the mother of the cousin I am telling you about."

Tess stared at him, wide eyed. Knowing what had happened to his wife, she couldn't help but feel a rush of sympathy for all that Guy had suffered. "That's just awful. I'm so sorry, Guy!"

Guy nodded and looked at her with eyes that pierced. He chuckled sardonically. "Yes, well, it was fine for my sister, but my cousin was not like me, you see. He was very—how do you say, feminine? He did not like to play boy games, and we did not get along, so my aunt, she did not like me. But my uncle was nice."

Guy got a faraway look, his eyes glassy with reminiscences. Then he shook his head.

"Anyway," he said, and opened his eyes wide, reaching across the table to hold her hand. "It was a long time ago."

Later, they strolled through Washington Square Park, and Guy told her about Paris. He talked about seeing his friends and playing soccer and going to cafés. Tess envied the sophisticated European lifestyle he had left behind. It was not so much the city itself but the community of friends and family he described that she wished she had.

They walked slowly along the dark paths, which were lit only by the gentle glow of old-fashioned street lights. Each lamp illuminated patches of grass, gardens, and children's play areas around it. Surrounding the park were beautiful turn-of-the-last-century town-homes, and massive brick buildings belonging to New York University. Fifth Avenue twinkled through the Washington Square Arch, and Tess wondered if it made Guy think of Paris and the Arc de Triomphe.

She had visited the city only once, when she was a student in Switzerland, but she and her friends had been far more interested in finding the best bar or party than in taking in the sights. She had only vague memories of the sprawling and historic metropolis that had struck her as surprisingly colorless—most of the buildings were white. She also remembered that it was cut in half by a canal. They had rode a ferry along it, Tess remembered, but her enjoymet of the view had been marred by a severe hangover.

Only a few people ambled past Tess and Guy now—on their way home or to some NYU gathering, Tess supposed, or perhaps to meet friends at a bar nearby. A single couple perched on the rim of the center fountain, kissing hesitantly, as if for the first time. Tess buttoned her coat, dipped her chin in its collar, and pushed her hands in her pockets for warmth.

After a while, they sat down on a bench, and Tess worked up the nerve to ask about Yves' mother. Even though she already knew the answer, she thought it would seem impolite not to ask, since he had asked her.

Guy peered up at the sky, blinking, and Tess wondered if it was to blink back tears. She pulled her hand from her pocket to squeeze his hand, regretting the question.

"I'm sorry!" she said. "You don't have to—"

"No, it's okay. It is natural you should ask me this question."

Tess bit her lip, grateful that the darkness at least partially obscured both their expressions.

He took a deep breath before beginning. "Her name was Marie," he said. "We met at the university. She was the first girl I truly loved. Before that time, when I dated girls, it was for different reasons. " He paused and smiled, shaking his head. "Not love. But with all my heart, I loved Marie.

"After she had Yves, I got a good job with this computer game company I am working for now. It was a lot of work, a lot of hours. We were not together all the time."

A dark cloud settled over him. "Marie became depressed. I thought it was because I was not there so much anymore. I did not know about this thing of women getting depressed after pregnancy. I thought it was just the circumstance, that she would get used to the new life and the new routine. I thought the money I was making would be worth it, and she would see that it would be good for our family."

He shook his head and breathed deeply. "Then—I didn't know the doctor had given her some pills for sleeping. He should not have done this because she was still feeding Yves from the breast. But one day I came home. She had taken all the pills. I could not wake her up."

He stopped speaking, and Tess swallowed, staring at him. Hot tears sprung to her own eyes as she again imagined Guy coming home to find his wife dead and his baby—Yves—where? Where would he have been? Asleep? Crying? Tess didn't have the courage to ask. She took Guy's hand. It felt cold and limp. He sat up but did not look at her.

She said, "That's horrible. I'm so sorry."

Guy smiled wanly. He jiggled her hand in his as if to lighten the mood. "You remind me of her. Not the way you look, but you have a similar heart. Like a person who cares."

Tess gulped but could not speak. She wondered briefly what Marie had looked like, thinking of Yves' face and the features that differed from Guy's. However they were arranged, she told herself, she was sure Marie was beautiful and sophisticated, like Guy. She imagined a chic European woman with a perfect body and confidant air.

A finger of insecurity wiggled up her spine, but then Guy leaned toward her and touched her cheek lightly, caressing it with his thumb. She was sure he could hear her heart sputtering in her chest, but he was as cool as the autumn air as he brushed a tress of hair behind her ear, ran his nose along the bridge of hers, and kissed her with a soft sweetness that made her head swim and her eyes shut of their own accord.

He pulled away after a moment, and she opened her eyes slowly, not wanting the kiss to end. When she did, she saw him looking at her with a mixture of sadness and sincerity.

"You are a very sensitive person," he said.

Tess's voice cracked unevenly when she spoke. "Thank you."

It felt like an inadequate answer, but Guy continued, "You do not belong here, though. I hope you do not mind me saying this."

Tess laughed softly. "I wish it weren't so obvious, but no, I don't really feel like I belong in New York." She took a deep breath. "I came down here from Canada with a boyfriend. He had just graduated business school, but there was a recession in Canada so no opportunities for him. He happened to have American citizenship through his father's side, so we took a chance and came here, thinking it would just be temporary."

She paused. "He did great. He's a really sweet guy and we're still friends, but it wasn't really meant to be more than that. I think I just thought I'd have this adventure and that would be it. But just after we broke up, I met my ex-husband, Patrick. I thought I was in love. We got pregnant, and the rest is pretty much history. Now we have joint custody, so I'm stuck here forever." She looked around tentatively, as if to assure herself that it was really true.

"Nothing is forever," Guy said. "You don't know what can happen."

Tess opened her eyes wide. "Oh!" She said aloud.

It suddenly occurred to her that Guy was right. She wouldn't, in fact, be stuck in New York forever. She would have a choice soon. She could leave.

A door burst open in her mind, and she wondered at the chill that blasted in from the other side.

CHAPTER 15

Halloween burst upon Cobble Hill like Mardi Gras in New Orleans. Clinton Street, in the bright orange of late afternoon, was thronged with children and parents in homemade costumes that looked like they had taken a weekend to create and assemble.

Rachel Shapiro struggled to keep up—and keep her composure—as the crowds pressed in on her. Tess glanced back at her apprehensively but needed to focus her attention on her children, who were scurrying from one stoop to the next, where clusters of costumed grownups sipped wine and laughed indulgently as they proffered their bowls of treats.

"Just a few more blocks," Tess called back to her. "If you get swallowed up, just phone me!"

Rachel raised a quelling hand, but Tess couldn't help but feel it was a mistake to bring her along on this excursion. She had aged since the last time Tess saw her. Since her husband's death, Rachel had maintained a thin physique and clad it in expensive designer clothes, but now the skin hung from her face and arms, and she looked like a fading soldier in battle, trying to take one last hill. Even her painstakingly dyed red hair now showed its white roots, and Tess wondered if it was fatigue or forgetfulness that had kept her from a trip to the salon before coming to New York City.

Tess jiggled the heart pendant on her necklace. She hated dressing up and now scuffed behind her children in worn jeans and brown clogs. Before leaving the house, her mother had eyed Tess's outfit critically and then, in response to Tess's warning eye, assured her that she "wasn't judging."

In front of her, Sammy rummaged through a bowl of candy with deliberation. Tess was about to scold him when he pulled out a package of Skittles—Rosie's favorite, not his. He ran up to his sister joyfully, his red superhero cape fluttering behind him, wielding his find and depositing it in her plastic pumpkin.

"Oh, *shank* you," Rosie managed through her vampire teeth.

They crossed the street, and Tess saw Patrick's yellow brick building in the middle of the block. He had set up two folding beach chairs and a card table between them, on which sat a bowl of candy. He was sitting on the nearer chair, and Tess strained to see if the chemo had caused any change in him. He didn't look weaker or thinner, and the hair on his head was the same. But as they approached and he stood up to greet them, she saw that his pallor was somewhat jaundiced, and there was a gleam of perspiration on his face, despite the cooler weather.

Even though she was at least a head shorter, Rachel managed an impressively intimidating air as she spoke to him in a clipped tone.

"Hello, Patrick," she said.

Patrick nodded. "Rachel."

Tess rolled her eyes. Patrick must be wondering if she had told her mother about his leukemia. Since she hadn't yet, and didn't want the encounter to become even weirder than it already was, she kissed the children and bid them good-bye.

Injecting cheer into her voice, she said, "Have fun handing out candy, you guys! I'll see you tomorrow after school, okay?"

They waved good-bye, and Tess led her mother down a side street so they could walk home on Court Street, which was a commercial avenue and so less crowded with trick-or-treaters. Her mother released a heavy sigh of relief.

"I had no idea it was going to be that crowded."

Tess looked at her sympathetically. "You look like you just want to go home and rest," she said. "Do you want to pick up some wine on the way back?"

In truth, Tess thought she could use a glass herself. It had been doubly stressful trying to keep an eye on her children while watching out for her mother. As they entered the brightly lit corner wine store near Tess's building, her phone buzzed. Tess's heart leapt when she saw it was a text from Guy.

What are you doing next weekend? Yves is going to spend Friday and Saturday night at the country house of a friend. Are you free? We could go away somewhere...

Tess groaned inwardly. She had seen Guy a few times since their first date, but because he had Yves full time, there was hardly a chance to stay out even past midnight. And now he was free for a whole weekend, and it had to be when Tess had her children!

Her mother appeared at her side with a bottle of Riesling. "What's wrong?" she asked.

Tess smiled. It was impossible to hide anything from her mother. She told her about Guy and the invitation. Her mother waved a hand and walked over to the cash register. As she handed over a twenty, she said, "Never mind, you're going."

Tess looked at her, confused. "Mom, I can't. I have the kids this weekend—and anyway, you're here!"

Her mother accepted her change, and the woman behind the register handed her the bottle in a brown paper bag.

"Exactly, I'm here," Rachel said. "We don't live in the same city, and I never have a chance to help you with the children like I always wanted. Now I have the opportunity. Text him back. Tell him you're going."

Tess looked at her, hesitating. "Are you sure you can handle—?"

"I can handle, I can handle. Now text him back."

Tess smiled and hugged her mother's thin frame. Then she typed a message on her phone and pressed send.

"Thanks, Mom."

The apartment normally felt lonely and empty when her children were away, but Tess now found it a relief to flop down on the sofa opposite her mother, her feet raised on an overturned cushion while Rachel rested hers on the coffee table. They sipped wine while the news murmured just audibly on the television. Tess knew Rachel had chosen the news because she had a crush on Anderson Cooper. She didn't have the heart to suggest they change channels or—God forbid—tell her mother that he was gay.

"He has such an intelligent look in his eyes, doesn't he?" Rachel asked.

Tess raised her eyebrows and nodded, drinking deeply from her wine glass to hide her smile.

After a moment of staring, Rachel said, "Is Patrick all right? He looked sick to me."

Tess swiveled her head. Really, her mother's intuitive powers were as astounding as her ability to mask her impressions! Tess took a deep breath and sat up, putting her feet on the floor. She reached over for the remote and muted the set.

"No," she said. "He's not."

Quietly, she told her mother about Patrick's leukemia and prognosis. Rachel looked on in stunned silence.

"Just a year?" she repeated.

Tess nodded.

"Tess, I'll be here. I'll be here for you. I'm going to come down more often. You'll need me, and so will the children."

Tess looked at her gratefully. "Okay. Thank you, Mom."

Her mother's eyes were glassy. "Those poor children! How much can they take?"

Tess bit her lip. "It's going to be rough."

"I always tried to protect you from anything like that," Rachel said. "I knew it could damage you. Children are so sensitive."

Tess looked at her, confused. She realized suddenly that her mother was drunk.

"Protect me? Protect me from what?"

Her mother looked startled, as if she didn't realize she'd spoken the words aloud. To Tess's horror, tears leaked out of the corners of her mother's eyes. Tess went to her and draped an arm around her mother's shoulders. But she couldn't suppress the burning question.

"Protect me from what?" she insisted.

Her mother looked down when she spoke. "I think your father was gay."

Tess pulled away from her. "No."

Her mother didn't look at her but rather sucked in a trembling bottom lip. When she spoke, her voice quaked with emotion. "I caught him one time, with some magazines…"

"No."

Tess felt every muscle in her body tense. This wasn't real. But her mother continued.

"And he…well, he was never really interested…"

Tess stood up, then felt a sudden flash of pain in her forehead. It was the same flash of discomfort she'd experienced when she was pregnant, so she knew what was coming. She bolted the bathroom and slammed the door, just making it to the toilet in time to retch torrents of wine.

When she was done, she flushed the toilet and sat with her back to the bathtub, wiping sweat from her forehead with her palm. She felt too weak to move. After a while her mother tapped softly on the door. She spoke in a quiet, scared voice.

"Tess? Tess, I'm so sorry!"

Tess shook her head. She stared at the ceiling. Was anything, anything in her life real? She swallowed and spoke in a voice just above a whisper.

"It's okay, Mom. It's really okay. You don't have to be sorry. *I'm* sorry."

CHAPTER 16

On Friday after school, Tess rushed to get Rosie and Sammy and then went home to pack.

Sammy was irritable. "I don't see why we have to stay with Grandma. Why can't we stay at Dad's?"

Tess had no answer for him. According to their divorce agreement, she had to tell Patrick when she was going away for more than six hours, in case he wanted to babysit the children. She had dutifully informed him, and he had e-mailed back that he had chemo on Thursday and would text her if he was feeling well enough. No answer had come, and she hadn't followed up. Truthfully, she would have felt terrible leaving her mother alone and purposeless in the apartment.

"Grandma said she'd take us to Build-A-Bear Workshop," Rosie said. "We're going in a taxi, and then she's taking us out to lunch at a fancy restaurant. Then on Sunday we're going to see *The Minions*."

"Oh, you'll have so much fun!" Tess said. "And you can call me anytime, okay?"

Sammy still groused. "I wish we could come to the convention with you."

Tess had told them she was going to a teacher's convention in New Jersey. She was still not sure why she had lied about the location. Guy was taking her to the Berkshires, but New Jersey had seemed such a typical destination for an educational conference that it had slipped out when she told them why she'd be away.

When they opened the door to the apartment, they were greeted with a waft of delicious cooking smells: chicken actually roasting in the oven and, she thought, potatoes with rosemary and garlic. Tess felt a wash of nostalgia for her childhood. In the dining room she saw Rachel had set three places for Shabbat dinner, dug out the challah from the freezer, and placed the candlesticks on either side.

She kissed Tess on the cheek and whispered in her ear, "Go pack. I've got everything under control."

And indeed she seemed to have tapped into some dormant energy source. For a moment she was the Rachel Shapiro of Tess's childhood. Tess felt a rush of warmth and gratitude and a sense that this was, somehow, the right thing for all of them.

When she bid the children good-bye, they clung to her extra tightly, but Tess could see from their smiles that they were not apprehensive. Rather, they seemed to be looking forward to the weekend. It made leaving so much easier.

The house Guy rented in Cobble Hill was a narrow brownstone with a steep flight of red painted stairs lined with pots of bare-branched plants. He opened the door a second after she knocked and grinned widely as he welcomed her in, grabbing her bag and hanging up her coat in one fluid motion.

Tess wandered hesitantly into the foyer and gasped.

"It's a museum!" she cried.

The main room was intricately decorated with wall moldings, oil paintings, brass and plaster statuettes, and rows of ancient-looking books on shelves to either side of the fireplace. In front of the bay windows, a shiny black grand piano twinkled under lamps with scalloped domes. In the middle of the room, under the rather stiff-looking sage-upholstered furniture, was an ornately woven Persian rug with a red background and Byzantium designs in yellow and royal blue.

Guy laughed and indicated a white, L-shaped desk that looked to be from Ikea at the far end of the room, covered with three different computer monitors and a stack of paperback manuals.

"That's the only thing that belongs to me," he said.

Tess laughed and looked at him. "It certainly stands out in contrast to all this."

His eyes were devilishly piercing, reflecting the gray of his T-shirt as he looked at her appraisingly. She had worn her most flattering jeans, tucked into a pair of brown leather boots, with a black V-neck sweater.

"Hi," she breathed and raised her head to kiss him.

He reached toward her with long, tapered fingers, which he traced down the side of her neck as he returned her kiss, sending shivers down her spine, and then opened his hand to gently hold the back of her neck as his kisses became more intense and purposeful. She turned her head to the side and gasped as he brought his hand under her sweater and gently caressed her breast with his thumb.

Pulling away, he took her hand and led her up the stairs to his bedroom, which was dark except for the shaft of a streetlight casting a shimmer of soft light over a half-made bed. A masculine smell, like cologne and worn shirts that still retained a whiff of laundry detergent, permeated the room. But the sheets were smooth, cool, and fresh feeling to her skin as he made love to her with slow control, seeming to sense it had been a while. She was surprised when she came, arching to meet him as he moaned in her ear. Usually she had to be with someone a few times before that happened, but her attraction to Guy was so magnetic; he seemed to fit her perfectly.

Afterward, they lay dozing while outside, darkness swept purple, then black, and a cold breeze shafted under the cracked window. Tess pulled the quilt over them and buried her face in his chest. He stroked her hair lightly until she fell into a deep sleep.

When she awoke, it was early morning, and Tess was famished. She sat up slowly, not wanting to wake Guy, but he reached up and pulled her to him. They made love again, and Tess half hoped they could just spend the weekend there, rather than driving to the mountains.

But Guy had no such thoughts as he looked at his watch on his nightstand. "*Merde*, we must leave soon," he said. "It takes three hours to arrive there."

Tess nodded and slid out of bed reluctantly.

"Are you hungry?" she asked.

Guy opened his eyes wide. "Starving. You take a shower and I will prepare breakfast."

By the time she got downstairs, Guy had toasted bagels and cut up fruit. She sat on a stool facing him at the gray marble island. He had made her coffee in the electric percolator, but shook his head when she asked if he was going to have a cup.

"I can't stand American coffee," he admitted, pulling a face. "In the morning I go out to buy an espresso."

Tess nodded, but she sipped her own cup gratefully. Between bites of bagel she asked, "So do you work mainly from home?"

She had imagined some cool warehouse setting filled with hoodie-clad computer geeks in their twenties, zipping between rows of desks on their skateboards.

Guy nodded. "Yes, I develop things here, and sometimes I go to the office in Tribeca." He paused and looked at her uncertainly. "Do you want to see something?"

Tess shrugged. "Okay, like what?"

Guy smiled mischievously and led her to his desk in the living room, carrying his plate with him. Tess brought her coffee. He leaned over and jiggled the mouse, and all three screens flickered to life. Then he set his plate down on the desk and took a seat in the padded black desk chair. Tess peered over his shoulder, watching as he clacked away on the keyboard until what she assumed was a computer game came on the middle screen. There was a video of two cars racing one another down FDR Drive, whizzing between the lanes, skirting the concrete divide, and occasionally crashing into fences or overshooting onto the promenade before skirting back.

Tess looked on, fascinated. "But when did they film this? I can see it's the middle of the day, but there aren't any other cars on the road. The traffic is always insane on the FDR."

Guy laughed. Then he slowly began removing layers of the image until Tess saw that the scene wasn't filmed at all, but rather computer-generated paintings of a sort—although they were as realistic as photographs—layered onto a green grid on top of a darker green background.

She gasped. "That's incredible. I had no idea computer simulation had become so sophisticated!"

She thought of her own illusions of making money off of her comic-book drawing skills and suddenly realized how foolish they were. The world had changed since that fateful night when she sat huddled behind a coat rack at the Hadassah Bazar. This was how animation was done nowadays. She could never hope to compete.

"Now watch this," Guy said, and he brought up another clip onto the screen.

In this scene, a blond woman in a gray suit was sitting in a chair by a crackling fire. She was being interviewed, but she was speaking in Russian or some other Eastern European language. Every so often, a balding, bespectacled reporter asked a question, and sometimes the camera would focus on his face for the reaction.

Tess said, "I don't understand it."

Guy didn't answer. Instead, he did the same thing he had done previously, stripping away the layers of artifice until Tess could see just a green graph of a figure, inclining and gesturing against a dark background.

Tess nearly choked on her coffee. "But that's impossible," she sputtered, coughing. "She seems so real. It all looked so perfectly real."

Guy swiveled around in his desk chair to face her, his face lit up in an elfish grin. He reached to take her cup from her hands and took a sip, then made a face.

"Ugh, American coffee! Like the toilet water. We'll have to stop someplace for a cappuccino."

Tess just stood there staring at him, shock rendering her unable to move. "I just…I never knew such technology existed."

He handed the cup back to her and smiled, waving his hands with a magician's flourish. "Now you know. You see, nothing maybe is really what you think. It could all be an illusion."

Tess thought bitterly of her mother's revelation of a few nights before. Is that what her whole childhood had been, an illusion? Her own marriage too. She bit her lip and looked off to the side.

Guy seemed not to notice her sudden change of mood as he turned off his computer and swiveled back around to look at her, his face begging a question.

"Can you do me a favor? I will shower and pack, and can you run to the coffee shop called La Provence and get me a double espresso cappuccino? I keep meaning to buy the machine for here, but..." He shrugged and let his voice trail off.

Tess snapped out of her reverie and nodded. "Of course!"

Outside a definite chill permeated the atmosphere. Tess shivered and zipped up her navy puffer jacket, feeling in the pockets for her gloves. An odd feeling, like waking from a bad dream only to realize you're still dreaming, took hold of her, and she shoved her gloved hands into her pockets and scuffed broodingly through the piles of dead leaves.

Weekend echoes of people sorting their trash and calling out to their neighbors floated through the shedding trees, like the disintegrating Halloween decorations half pulled from homes and shrubbery.

She felt slightly cheered standing in line at La Provence. The unfinished wooden floor and cheerful red-checked tablecloths created a cozy, inviting atmosphere, and the smell of fresh espresso beans percolating behind the counter made Tess feel like she had stepped into a tiny corner of Europe.

As Tess stood in line behind the pastry-filled counter, Stephanie—a one-time close friend whom she now saw less due to work and different schools—got up from a table where she was having breakfast with her family and greeted her warmly. Tess turned in surprise, her face lighting up with a smile as she gave her old friend a quick embrace. Stephanie stood back and appraised her.

"You look great," she said. "Did you lose weight or something?"

Tess nodded and said with slight chuckle, "All one hundred and seventy pounds that I chucked out after the divorce."

Stephanie's smile disappeared, and Tess immediately regretted the brusqueness of her remark.

"I'm sorry," she said. "I thought everyone knew."

Stephanie shook her head, her eyebrows knitted in concern. "Are you serious? You're divorced?"

Tess took a deep breath, guilt a steam valve pressuring her to launch into the explanation she felt no desire to give. Not now. Instead, she shrugged and said, "It's okay, honestly. It was a while ago." She added, trying to change the subject, "You look great too, by the way."

And she did, Tess thought. Stephanie was a marathon runner, and even in a bulky sweatshirt, her athlete's body radiated strength and energy, and her cheeks glowed with health under her short black hair.

But her eyes were still filled with a heartfelt sympathy that made Tess's insides twinge with agitation. Then, a loud clatter and cry sounded from Stephanie's table, and she turned to see that her youngest had dropped her plate of food on the floor—cut-up bits of French toast splayed out on the floor beneath him.

"Oh!" Stephanie looked at Tess, but her face was contorted with the conflicting urges to continue the conversation or return to her family.

"I'm okay, really!" Tess assured her, feeling relieved.

Stephanie paused but then nodded, and Tess held out her arms for another quick embrace. "It was good to see you," she said.

"I'm going to e-mail you," Stephanie said, before turning back to her table, where a waiter now stood with a broom. It sounded like a warning.

Tess smiled and called after her. "Yes, let's get together."

Walking back to Guy's place, the warmth from the cup permeating her gloved hand, Tess wondered if she was actually okay, as she had told Stephanie. It was so odd, what Guy had just shown her, but it was more than that…Something niggled from far away—something about things not being quite what they seemed.

She chewed her lip, ruminating on the idea. It was perhaps, she decided, just the echo of the façade of her parents' marriage, and her own. You think everything is one way, but then one morning someone oversleeps and forgets to lower the backdrop scenery on the stage of your life, and you realize that it's all an illusion.

She pondered this idea even as she reentered Guy's home and handed him his coffee, which he drank gratefully in the living room. Then, before she knew it, they were seated in a shiny black Audi, which Guy had rented for the weekend, and speeding up the West Side Highway.

It had turned into a perfect fall day, like a crisp red apple, and the raspy-sweet French melodies Guy had brought to play for her on the road melted away her earlier uncomfortable feelings, like fallen leaves blown to the side of the road by a speeding car. In stolen glances, she took in Guy's profile, outlined against the backdrop of the Hudson River and a crystal-blue sky: handsome, confident, and happy. His happiness made her happy too, because she felt it must be, in some part, because of her.

CHAPTER 17

As they approached their destination, Tess admired the civilized calm of the Berkshires: softly rolling hills and subtly tamed nature; farms with quaint open-air stands where they sold the goods that—she thought cynically—hadn't yet been picked up by the local supermarket; and green meadows, turning to brown, which she imagined covered in wildflowers in spring and summer.

While undeniably beautiful, the nature around her still compared unfavorably against the wild, unrestrained beauty of the Canadian Pacific Northwest where she had grown up, and she felt a pang of longing for home. There, nature was all powerful: ancient ferns that peaked to the heavens with soft, newly formed moss; waterfalls that crashed into pools and tumbled into rivers; and mammoth mountains that pierced her soul.

The bed and breakfast in Stockbridge was a shimmering white edifice that looked like it had once been a grand mansion. Behind it, a wave of tree-covered mountains seemed to extend endlessly in either direction. Tess imagined that, a month earlier, the autumn foliage must have made this a breathtaking sight. Now a few colored leaves still clung to the trees, but they had mostly fallen, leaving thin fingers of branches which clawed the sky.

Guy cut the engine and sagged comically onto the steering wheel.

"We have arrived," he said wearily.

Tess looked at his tired face and felt a stab of guilt. "You should have given me a turn to drive."

Guy perked up. "Ah, it is fine, really. I like to drive."

As if to counter his last impression, he hopped out of the car and popped the trunk, hauling out their bags before Tess had fully extracted herself from the front seat. She inhaled sharply. The sweet smack of fresh air always made her wistful upon leaving the city, uncoiling knots she didn't know she had and enlivening senses she'd long forgotten. She looked at Guy, smiled broadly, and then yanked her own bag from his shoulder.

"Let me," she insisted. "I can tell you're beat."

Inside the front entrance, it looked to Tess like the editors of *Bed and Breakfast Magazine* had spewed the remnants of a Laura Ashley photo shoot into the front parlor. Doilies and patterned curtains abounded, and a small fire crackled lazily in an adjoining common room. She smiled to herself and then set down her bag and peered around while Guy went off in search of the owner.

While he was gone, she perused the shelves in the living room, which were stacked with paperbacks and board games interspersed with framed photos: A middle-aged couple Tess assumed to be the owners, and two college-aged boys who looked like they must be their children.

Her suppositions were proved at least partially correct when Guy reappeared with a man he introduced as Norman, their host, who shook her hand with vigor. He was keen to suggest that guests could gather in the den in the evening to play board games, nibble snacks, and socialize with one another.

Tess felt a pang of pity for him, intuiting his fantasy for the life he and his wife had probably left the city for. But she had other plans for her evening with Guy. These were heightened when Norman showed them their room.

"It's small," he said apologetically. "But it has this wonderful gas fireplace. Some guests prefer to turn off the heat and sleep with the fireplace on."

He demonstrated by flicking off the light turning the adjacent knob for the fireplace. Immediately, the room was filled with a warm orange glow, and it heated up considerably.

They thanked him, and he left them to unpack their things. Tess sent a quick text to her mother to let her know they had arrived safely and then hastily unpacked her things into an artfully distressed dresser.

"Should we find somewhere to eat?" Guy suggested.

Tess felt a tad disappointed that this would be the first thing they would be doing—but they had all night, she reminded herself. At Norman's suggestion, they went to the Bear Inn and had meat pies and salad. Guy drank beer and Tess had hard cider, which made her feel mellow and ready to crawl under the perversely inviting white duvet back in their room. But she looked at Guy and his keen expression, and she could tell he was more interested in exploration and adventure.

By the time they got out of the pub, however, evening was approaching. Tess had forgotten that it got dark earlier in the mountains. With the lessening of light, the quiet became more apparent, and Tess shivered as an aggressive chill nipped at the tip of her nose and frosty fingers slid through the loose weave of her brown woolen sweater. She zipped her coat and pulled on a woolen hat had she had crammed in her jacket pocket.

Guy buttoned his pea coat and buried his hands in its pockets. He smiled at the mountains; dark-green shadows encircled by descending light.

"Should we at least try and see a little nature? It's an awkward hour, but maybe we can go for a walk?"

Tess looked down at her navy Puma sneakers; she had forgotten to change into her hiking boots before they'd left. But Guy's confidence and enthusiasm were irresistible. She slid her hand under his arm and said, "Sure!" with more eagerness than she felt.

In truth she thought they would just walk along a path by a stream for an hour and then go check out the town. When they got in the car, however, Guy fiddled with the GPS, and then they drove a little ways before pulling over to the side of the road. Tess read the wooden sign posted next to a path that curved into the distance

"Guy, this is a hike. We'll never make it before it gets dark, and we don't have the right shoes or flashlights..." She felt her panic rising, but a glance at Guy's ever-cool demeanor caused her to bite her lip. They got out of the car.

Guy pointed at the sign. "You see, it says it's *easy*. Forty minutes at most."

Tess nodded but looked up at the sky, wondering if they actually had forty minutes before it was pitch black outside.

"I'm just not sure…" she began, nodding toward the darkening sky.

Guy laughed and pulled her to the trail's entrance, a dark mouth between the trees.

"It will be fine," he said. "I will protect you."

They began the climb up the marked trail, Guy taking it in easy, long-legged strides and Tess trying to hurry without appearing to do so. It was dark between the dense shrouds of trees on either side, and she was glad Guy couldn't see her cheeks redden with alarm as fear tightened her jaws.

Guy plowed ahead, unruffled. After twenty minutes of hard climbing, Tess felt overjoyed to see that they had in fact reached a summit of sorts—a large expanse of flat rock—that offered stunning vistas of the surrounding valley and mountains. The purple sky was decorated by streams of migrating birds and smoky descents of clouds. A pine-filled campfire smell permeated the air, and she inhaled deeply. It was a magical view, and she felt grateful to Guy for bringing her there. Her earlier feelings of foreboding seemed foolish to her now.

She wished she could be more easygoing, like Guy. People like her missed out on views like these because they were afraid, and now…She sighed. The world really was a glorious place. She looked up at Guy, whose expression mirrored her own feelings, and she took his hand and squeezed it.

Surprisingly it was he who now said, "It's so beautiful, but it's getting late. We should turn back."

Tess nodded, but despite his words, Guy walked with easy, slow strides to the other side of the summit, looking for the continuation of the trail that would lead down the mountain they had just ascended. After searching for several moments, he shook his head and looked at her.

"I can't see where it is marked," he said.

Tess walked to where he stood, her eyes searching each tree for a yellow streak of paint. She gritted her teeth in annoyance.

"It's not here."

For once Guy furrowed his brows in concern. "We will have to go back down the way we came."

Tess didn't need to be told twice. It was growing seriously dark now, and she headed directly to the outgrowth of trees from which they had come. Guy followed as she marched forward, her eyes on the ground to avoid tripping over rocks or branches.

Every so often she glanced up, trying to find a marker, but it was hopeless. The paint was on the other side of the trees. She plunged forward, hoping for the best and grateful once again that Guy could not see her. Tears welled up in her eyes as she imagined the next day's news articles: "Bed-and-breakfast owner Norman Fikelstein was quoted as saying he became alarmed when the couple didn't return in time for the eight o'clock game of charades, for which they had expressed avid interest."

She was aware of Guy's plodding footsteps behind her, even and devoid of the frantic feeling that rose like a disturbed rattlesnake from her chest and coiled around her throat. After a while she was sure she'd taken the wrong turn. That steep incline of rock hadn't been there on the way up.

Guy looked at it. "Are you sure we are going the right way?"

Tess wheeled on him. "No!" she cried. "I don't know where we are. The markers are on the wrong side of the trees because this is the way up. We were supposed to come down the other way. I think we're lost."

She began to sob. *Dammit.*

Guy held her and stroked her cheeks where the tears had been streaming down for the past ten minutes, much to her chagrin because she hadn't wanted him to know she wasn't cool like him; wasn't unafraid.

"It's okay," he whispered. "We'll find our way back. I'm sorry, so sorry. I didn't realize you were scared."

Tess released a shuddered breath and let Guy lead the way. Amazingly, his confidence was justified. He held her hand as she slid with as much composure as possible down the steep rock face, and led her through paths that intersected but clearly weren't a part of one another, until by some otherworldly miracle, they stepped out onto the road.

Guy pointed uphill to the right. "I think we are parked down there."

Tess heaved with relief. Immediately, she forgot the distress of moments before, like she had almost been hit by a car but wasn't. But her embarrassment over her emotional outburst lingered, and they drove in silence toward the town. Guy stole a glance at her.

"Um, do you want to go to the town center?"

Tess shook her head. "I think I just want to go back."

Guy shrugged and inclined his head. "We might get hungry later."

Tess pleaded, "Oh can't we just pick up some snacks at a gas station or something?"

Guy frowned and nodded. They stopped at a Seven Eleven and bought bread, peanut butter, yogurts, and some waxy-looking fruit from the counter near the cash register. It was darkest night by the time they got out, and Guy's headlights pierced the blackness as they careened through the narrow mountain roads. Tess pressed her forehead up against the cool glass beside her and peered into the dark.

When they entered the main floor of the B & B, they were greeted by sounds of enthusiastic voices, rolling dice, and game pieces tocking noisily on cardboard surfaces. An assortment of guests clustered around different tables, playing Scrabble, Yahtzee, and Farkle with audible enthusiasm. Norman's wife, a comfortably middle-aged woman in a flowing purple smock dress, beckoned them to join.

"We have snacks and wine!" She indicated a side table with red wine in a glass decanter, and plates of fruit, crackers, cheese, and cookies.

Tess pulled her Seven Eleven bags behind her back. "We've eaten," she lied, "but thank you." She looked at Guy, who was eyeing her sympathetically.

"I think we'll turn in. We went for a hike and we're pretty tired."

Mrs. Finkelstein smiled knowingly and gave them a wink. "Okay, have a good night," she said. "Breakfast is between eight and ten thirty."

Tess entered their room, and Guy shut the door behind them. He immediately began kissing her tenderly, holding her face between his palms. She let the bags slide to the floor, not caring that she heard an apple roll somewhere in the direction of the bed.

He guided her there in sure but gentle moves, and she willingly shuffled backward until she was on top of the covers, Guy pausing to pull off her turtleneck and unhook her bra.

He took his time with her, like the first time, and she couldn't help but feel a little selfish. But it all seemed to flow so perfectly, so magically. There wasn't really an opportunity for her to change positions or do anything but let this beautiful man make love to her. And in truth, it was all he seemed to want to do. How did she get so lucky all of a sudden?

They drifted off to sleep, her face turned away this time and Guy's hand resting lightly on her shoulder.

The gesture reminded her paradoxically of Patrick coming up behind her in the kitchen, resting his hands on her shoulders, and speaking smoothly in her ear: "Hey I've got plans tonight and tomorrow, but if you need me home for bedtime tomorrow night, I can cancel that one. It's not as important."

Baby, high chair, crying. "Um, no, it's okay, you go have fun."

Dumbass. She drifted off into a disgruntled sleep.

CHAPTER 18

The room was pitch black and freezing. Tess's feet felt numb as she tiptoed to the dresser and pulled her pajamas on soundlessly. Still cold, she padded over to the wall next to the door, where Norman had shown them the round knob for the fireplace. She eased it on slowly, until a warm, low glow emanated from the fireplace. Then she scurried back to nestle under the covers, her feet accidentally treading against the bags of food she'd let drop earlier on her way. She froze for an instant, glancing at Guy to make sure she hadn't woken him, but he slept on peacefully. Men, she thought. Never cold.

But when she got back under the covers, he grabbed her with a suddenness that made her yelp. He covered her mouth with his hand and whispered, "Shh-sh!" into her ear. "You'll wake the other guests!"

Only when he felt her relax did he release his grip. She laughed at his genuinely scared expression.

"I'm sorry," she said. "I was cold!"

Guy nodded and fell back onto his pillows, laughing too. "What time is it?"

Tess picked up her phone, charging on the nightstand next to her. "After midnight," she said.

Guy nodded. "We didn't have dinner. Are you hungry?"

It took Tess a moment to realize that she was, in fact, quite hungry. "I'll turn on the light," she offered, and snapped on a lamp on her bedside table.

She brought the bags to the bed, stooping to fish out the lost apple from where it rested in between the folds of the ruffled bed curtain, and dumped the entire contents of both bags onto the bed. Together they spread peanut butter onto bread with their fingers and bent the aluminum foil lids of their yogurts to use as spoons.

"This is disgusting," Guy said, and laughed.

Afterward they gathered up the trash and put it in the bags, tying them up securely before placing them by the door, and then dove back under the covers to sleep soundly for several more hours—until a blast of late-morning light awoke them both like a trumpet call.

They moaned and attempted to bury their heads but eventually sat up. Guy yawned and forced his eyes open wide.

"Did you see the shower yet?"

Tess shook her head, rubbing her eyes, and Guy smiled impishly and inclined his head for her to go into the bathroom and look.

Lined with stone-colored tiles, the shower stall was the size of a walk-in closet and featured benches and several shower heads. The floor, she was impressed to note, had begun to warm up under her feet since she turned on the light switch.

"It's a spa!" she proclaimed when she ermerged.

"And we are here to treat ourselves," Guy intoned.

He rose and gently took her by the wrist, leading her back into the bathroom, where he turned on all the nozzles in the shower, testing the temperature before pulling her in.

It was like being in a Swedish rain forest. Tess drifted from one over-sized nozzle to the next, letting the warm rivulets pound, stream, and tickle her according to their various settings. Guy watched her, then picked up a bar of soap and lathered it between his palms before rubbing it all over her. He massaged mint shampoo into her scalp and held her hair straight out behind her, letting water course through it and run in soapy streams down the drain.

Then it was her turn. Working the soap into a thick lather, she reached up to his shoulders and massaged him, working down his back until he moaned, closed his eyes, and sat on one of the stone benches just sideways enough for her to work her hands to the base of his spine, the tops of his buttocks. He turned, leaning up against the wall, and she paused to look at him, his perfect body relaxed and ready for her to please him this time, using her mouth on every part of him until he came with a deep, animal groan that caused her insides to shift.

Afterward, Guy emerged from the bathroom first, while Tess took time to use the hair dryer. When she came out, a fluffy pink towel tucked around her middle, Guy was already dressed in jeans and a black T-shirt, his feet bare, staring at the TV. His expression was rapt but emotionless, and Tess glanced at the set.

A male reporter with black glasses and a yellow scarf spoke with a British accent on what appeared to be a London street. Behind him were ambulances, police cars, and police officers. The crawler at the bottom of the screen announced: "London in state of emergency as police hunt for NAFKA terrorists who opened fire inside French cultural center Friday."

Tess stared at it in horror.

"Turn it up," she said.

Guy pressed the remote, and Tess listened to the reporter explain how the terrorists had easily gained access to the building, which was open to the public, and opened fire on a floor containing mostly office workers.

"At this time, it is confirmed that eight people are wounded and one killed. Police are conducting house-to-house searches in the London suburb of Richmond, where they believe the terrorists were based."

Footage of police entering homes, and startled residents waiting on porches or front lawns, played out on the screen.

"Holy fuck," Tess said. "I can't believe we missed this yesterday."

Guy nodded. "It is amazing, yes."

Then the screen was filled by a videotaped statement by the French prime minister, standing at a podium, a row of flags behind him. He spoke in French, but in a moment the volume on his voice was dimmed as the same British reporter translated his words.

"That was the French prime minister speaking earlier this morning, calling on the German government to find and eradicate these cowards, these criminals. He is pointing the finger squarely at the German chancellor and saying it is her responsibility to rid the world of this threat."

Tess said, "That's what my mother said."

"What is?"

"That it's the German government's responsibility. She thinks they're letting this happen."

Guy shrugged. "It would not be the first time."

Tess grinned. "She said that too."

The reporter continued, "We understand that at this time the German chancellor has issued a response, accusing France of hypocrisy, both moral and bureaucratic, as it has failed to respond to the pleas of victims of radical Islam in its former colonies."

Guy turned off the TV. "That is enough," he said. "We are still on holiday."

Tess frowned. "But, Guy, France should accept those refugees, shouldn't she? I mean, they have nowhere to go."

Guy raised one shoulder. "It is easy to say this from a country as big as America or Canada," he said. "But France, she is *toute petite.*" He made the symbol for *tiny* with his thumb and index finger. "We do not have room for so many refugees."

Tess bit her lip but didn't say anything. She didn't want to argue about politics here and now with Guy.

He echoed her sentiments and held both of her hands lightly in his. "Hey, forget it, okay? Let's just enjoy ourselves."

Tess nodded and smiled. "I know," she said. "I guess I take that kind of stuff too personally sometimes."

They made it downstairs in time to join the other guests for smoked salmon and bagels, fresh fruit and strong coffee, which even Guy forced himself to drink, wincing as he swallowed but saying he needed the caffeine for the drive home.

Norman looked pleased to see everyone eating and chatting with one another. Dressed in a maroon sweater and pleated khakis, his fringed bald head gleaming, he smiled and shook their hands as they left.

"Have a safe trip!" he said, before shutting the door.

Once outside, Guy took a deep breath. "Well, we have a few hours, is there anything we can do?"

Tess suggested the Norman Rockwell Museum, and on the way there she explained who the artist was. It wasn't much of a place, she thought. More like a brightly lit wooden cabin with some pictures of Rockwell's iconic magazine covers hanging on the walls, but she did like them. She could tell Guy was unimpressed, however, and she realized there was nothing about them that would resonate with him. It was pure Americana. It occurred to her that, at the time these idealized depictions of middle class American life were created, France would still have been digging herself out of World War Two.

Afterward they drove home in comfortable silence. The day had turned cloudy and Tess peered out at the grayness. Gradually, the car lulled her to sleep, and—despite her insistence that he let her drive halfway—they had already pulled up in front of her building when he nudged her awake.

She jerked awake and groaned. "You shouldn't have let me sleep."

"I wanted to. You needed it."

Tess sighed. He was right, she supposed. The next day was Monday and a full week of work ahead. Impossible to come out of this dream world and enter the real one so quickly!

She said, "Thank you. I had a wonderful weekend."

Guy smiled and ran his thumb across her cheek. "Even though I made you scared on the hike?"

Tess smiled and nodded. "Yes," she said. "It taught me to trust you."

CHAPTER 19

Tess stared at the alarm clock. Twelve thirty and she was still awake. She blamed the long nap in the car. Sitting up, she flicked on the lamp by her bed and pulled her knees up to her chest. Happy feelings about her weekend with Guy filled her thoughts, and she glanced at the empty spot beside her in bed, wishing he was there.

Gradually, her eyes adjusted to the light. The drawer in her nightstand contained a spiral notebook of drawing paper and some sharpened pencils. Like a feckless addict she began to sketch a story that, for the first time in a long time, had nothing to do with Patrick.

Relief and relaxation flowed through her as her pencil imprinted a story line that was more in keeping with her former tales. Andrea Chambers was dressed in a close-fitting black turtleneck and a pea coat as she confidently navigated the steep incline of forest in high-heeled boots. She paused and ducked behind a tree, peering behind her. Her pursuers were close—too close. Deftly, she climbed the tree and balanced in the curve of a branch as they passed unwittingly beneath her. From its height she spied a big wooden house, round and modern—a contradiction to the nature that surrounded it. She must reach it, somehow, before the surly team that tracked her.

Tess was feeling good, now. She tapped the eraser on the page, thinking about what would happen next. From the living room, the bell tone of her cell sounded loudly. Alarmed, she hurried out to answer it, afraid that it would wake her mother, who was asleep in Rosie's room and needed to wake up early to catch her flight.

A woman's voice, clear and businesslike, came through the phone.

"Good evening, Ms. Shapiro. My name is Carole Cassidy. I'm calling from St. Luke's Roosevelt Hospital. I just wanted to let you know that your ex-husband, Patrick Faygel, has been admitted into care. He arrived in our emergency room this evening. He asked us to call you."

A dull roar filled Tess's ears as she dashed to her desk to find a pen and paper to write down any pertinent information. "I don't understand. Patrick was supposed to be undergoing chemotherapy. He wasn't supposed to be going downhill so fast."

There was a muffled conversation that Tess couldn't understand. It sounded as though Nurse Cassidy had covered the mouthpiece while conferring with someone. After a moment she spoke again.

"I'm afraid Mr. Faygel refused chemo, Ms. Shapiro. I'm not sure where you got that information."

Tess's voice was ice. "I got that information from him."

The nurse cleared her throat. "Here's Dr. Friedman."

After a muffled pause a man's voice blundered onto the line.

"Mrs. Faygel?"

Tess swallowed. "Shapiro," she corrected. "We're divorced."

"I see…" He paused to clear his throat before continuing. "I'm sorry," he said. "I don't think he's coming out. We're going to do everything we can for him in here, but after that he's probably going to get transferred to palliative."

His words were a sickening blow. Tess covered the mouthpiece and tried to control her voice before she spoke again. "He told me he was getting chemo. He said he had a year."

Dr. Friedman released an exasperated sigh that made Tess ripple with anger. Why had she believed Patrick? When had he ever told the truth?

Dr. Friedman said simply, "No. I'm sorry."

Tess swallowed and went over to sit on the sofa. "How long?"

Rosie's door, which opened off the living room, creaked open and Rachel appeared in the doorway, wearing a floral cotton nightdress and looking at Tess with rapt concern. Tess eyed her as the doctor spoke.

"We can't say exactly, but maybe a month, maybe two. We'll do what we can for him here, then there's a facility nearby where we'll keep him comfortable. It will be easier for the family to visit him there, and I would imagine less disturbing for the children."

Tess swallowed. "Can I bring the children to see him tomorrow?"

"Yes, that's actually why we're calling you now. He's asked to see the children in the morning, if possible."

Tess nodded. "Yes, okay."

She wrote down the details of Patrick's location and hung up. Rachel Shapiro came to her side and hugged her daughter.

"What happened?" she asked.

But Tess could not speak. She was overcome by a swell of sobbing, and it took her several moments to calm down. Finally, she took a deep, tremulous breath and told her mother what the doctor had said.

Her mother nodded slowly. "I'm canceling my flight."

Tess started to object but relented. She knew her mother wouldn't change her mind, and anyway, she didn't want to be alone in the morning when she told the children; didn't want them to have to deal with the double blow of the terrible news about Patrick, and Grandma leaving.

While her mother spoke softly on the phone, Tess e-mailed the principal and secretary at work to let them know that she would be absent and explained the reason why. Then she e-mailed her children's school.

When she finished her call, her mother came over and patted Tess's shoulder. "Go get some rest, doll. You're going to need it."

Telling the children in the morning was every bit as difficult as Tess had feared. They were sitting at the table with Rachel, spooning cereal into their mouths, when she sat down to speak with them. They stopped eating to listen, and although Tess omitted the detail about Patrick only having a few months at most, they were bewildered and upset to hear that he was in hospital, and Tess could see from their faces that they sensed something was very wrong.

Rosie still clutched her spoon in her hand and her grip was so tight that her thumb and index finger had turned white.

She said, "But why did he need to go to the hospital at night? He told us he goes in the day. Then he comes home."

Tess smoothed her hair. "Last night he felt very sick and so he took a taxi to the hospital. They want to keep him there for a while and see what they can do to make him feel better."

"But will he feel better?"

Tess was at a loss for words. She looked across at her mother who said, "We don't know, but they're going to do everything they can to help him."

Sammy leaned over to rest his head on his grandmother's arm. His eyes held a faraway expression that made Tess's stomach ripple with anguish. He was too young, she thought. This was too much.

They abandoned their soggy cereal bowls and went instead to eat breakfast at a neighborhood diner where Tess told the children they could have anything they wanted, even juice with pancakes or French toast, which she didn't normally allow due to the double dose of sugar.

The lobby of the hospital was a pandemonium of activity—patients and visitors sitting on vinyl chairs, doctors and nurses rushing in and out, a bustling gift shop, and a line of people waiting to speak to someone behind the information desk.

Fortunately, Tess knew from speaking to the nurse where to go, and she led her family to the elevators and up to a floor that was shockingly still and quiet in contrast to the main floor below. A long reception desk took up most of the center space of the corridor, and bright sunlight streamed through windows on one side, making Tess inexplicably queasy and wishing it were a cloudy day to suit their moods.

She approached one of the nurses behind the desk, who pointed her in the direction of Patrick's room. Before they entered, she spoke to the children in a quiet voice.

"Now remember: If Daddy's asleep, just tiptoe inside quietly. There are probably chairs to sit in, and we can wait there for him to wake up."

They nodded silently, and she paused at the entrance to his room. Seeing him there, she realized suddenly she wasn't sure she was ready for her children to see this: Patrick's form sunken on the hospital bed, his skin sallow in the bright sunlight, an arsenal of equipment beeping and pumping through tubes and wires attached to his body—Rosie's greatest nightmare sprung to life.

But then Patrick turned, his head flopping to face them like a heavy rock being heaved over. He looked at them with half-opened eyes, and Tess could tell he was trying to move his features into a welcoming expression.

"Daddy." Rosie's voice sounded shocked and full of breath. Thin tears sprung to her eyes and leaked down her cheeks.

Sammy howled, and Tess lifted him up in a tight hug.

"It's okay," she said, again and again, unconsciously jiggling him like she would a much younger child.

She carried Sammy over to the window to distract him with the view, while Rosie stayed rooted to the spot, just inside the doorway.

Tess pointed. "Look, you can see the whole city from here!" She indicated the different famous buildings and asked if Sammy knew their names.

Then she heard Patrick's voice. "Rosie, it's okay. I just woke up. Come to Daddy."

Tess turned, and Sammy's wails subsided at the sound of Patrick's voice. But Rosie was crying now, repressed hiccups bubbling through her tightly pressed lips like steam raising the lid off a pot, as she stood next to Patrick's bed. Tess bit her lip and carried Sammy closer.

"I'm just groggy from all the medicine."

Patrick's voice sounded rough and exhausted. Rosie, beside him now, nodded - apparently not trusting herself to speak.

But Sammy cried, "Daddy, are you going to die?"

Patrick looked at him. "Who's not going to die?"

Sammy's brow furrowed with confusion. "I mean now."

Patrick blinked and swallowed. His voice came out scratchy and uneven.

"Soon, yes."

Tess thought Sammy was going to renew his loud cries, but he just snuffled quietly, his eyes on Patrick.

"Can I hug you, Daddy?"

Weakly, Patrick raised his arms from the elbow only. Tess saw they trembled, and she quickly and gently placed Sammy beside him on the bed to hide the fact. Sammy put his arms around Patrick, and Rosie joined the hug. Tess took a step backward. The darkness of death spread like black smoke, seeping into her and coating her insides.

What had she said to him, once? "On your deathbed—maybe on your deathbed—you'll understand what you did."

Looking at Patrick now, embracing his children, Tess thought that was probably the last thing he was considering. And she also realized that, without knowing it, she had somehow come to accept the fact that remorse was not part of Patrick's emotional software. Like love. He had never felt it, never really understood it. Looking at him hugging his children, she knew a stranger would not believe this pronouncement, but Tess knew the truth.

She felt ugly as she forced herself to remember horrid examples. Patrick had had unprotected sex with her when she was pregnant, even after being with some crackhead hooker after work that day. And then, after she'd discovered the whole truth and offered him friendship and support, and even an amicable divorce, Patrick had refused to leave, even though he had already rented another apartment. He chose, instead, to stay and date other women openly, taking obvious pleasure in her suffering. She pushed these thoughts into her consciousness and tried to cling to the anger. But she still felt sad.

Patrick spoke to her. "The hospital called my family."

Tess took a deep breath and nodded. "Will they be coming here?"

Patrick nodded with visible effort. "They're making arrangements."

Tess felt sick with the thought of seeing Patrick's family. For ten years they'd told her they loved her, had brandished their superior good-Christian image in front of her. Then, when Patrick refused to leave the apartment, she saw texts and e-mails from them encouraging him to stay, regardless of the misery he was inflicting on her. They expressed not even a single kind word or thought about her. Like her relationship with Patrick, it seemed that every pleasant interaction with his family had been tinged with fakery.

Finally she said, "Okay, guys. I think Daddy is tired. We'll come back tomorrow, okay?"

Patrick loosened his grasp so the children could slide out, protesting.

Sammy said, "I want to stay here, with Dad!"

Tess said, "I know, sweetie. But we'll come back lots and lots. We have to do what the doctor says is best for Daddy right now."

"So he can get better?" Sammy asked, hopefully.

The smile froze on Tess's face.

"Yes, Sammy," Rosie said.

And Tess looked at her gratefully: her big, grownup girl.

CHAPTER 20

"**B**ut I don't understand why you are so upset."

Guy was sitting on the floor of his living room, having just taken a giant toke of a joint. He spoke with his breath sucked in, and passed the cigarette to Tess, who was sitting beside him with her legs stretched out in front of her, ankles crossed. As they talked, she glanced frequently at her watch, wanting to be sure she was long gone before Yves returned from the birthday party he was attending. Two thirty, still two hours to go until he was dropped off back home. She held the joint between her fingers, looking at it.

"I don't know either," she admitted and took a long pull and also spoke with her breath held. "Patrick was so awful at the end, so cruel. Do you know what he did on my birthday?"

Guy shook his head, and Tess exhaled before passing it back.

"I didn't have big plans or anything. I was just going to meet a neighbor across the street for a drink. It was a horrible time, and I didn't feel like celebrating." She paused. "Anyway, that morning, Patrick said on his way out the door: 'Sammy peed the sheets in the night. I left the sheets in the bathtub for you to wash. I'll be home late. I have a date.' Then he left."

"*Merde,*" Guy said softly, shaking his head.

Tess grimaced, remembering. "I said I'd bolt the door, and later that day I got an e-mail from his lawyer saying that if I bolted the door, he had instructed his client to call the police and have them knock the door down. In front of his children. He was willing to do that in front of his own children."

"What an asshole! Shit, Tess, you should be glad he's dying! Be glad he's suffering!"

Tess smiled weakly. "I guess it's closure. I still want closure—an apology or something. I don't know. I still struggle to come to terms with the fact that I was duped for ten years—that I loved someone who didn't love me back. And that he was willing to continue to pretend, and let me continue to be confused and depressed for the rest of my life. He was willing to do all that to me."

Guy heaved a sigh. "I don't understand this. I don't understand how someone could not love you."

Tess gazed at him adoringly, her breath catching in her throat. But they weren't saying that, she knew. This was an affair, a fling.

She leaned over and kissed him. When she pulled away, he exhaled a puff of smoke and they both laughed. It felt good to lighten the mood. Guy gently stubbed out the joint in the ashtray and turned to her, cupping her chin as he kissed her.

They made love on the patterned rug in the living room, Tess relaxed and dreamy from the pot, but Guy more aggressive than usual, as if he wanted something from her. His cry at the end was deep and personal and left Tess feeling remote, as if she could have been anyone. But she put it down to the weed.

She whispered in his ear, "I should go. It's getting late."

Guy rolled off her and onto his back. His chest rose and fell with the erratic beating of his heart.

"Are you working tomorrow?"

Tess shook her head as she pulled on her jeans. "The principal told me to take a leave of absence. They got a substitute, but I'm still going to pop in now and again."

In truth, the e-mail from Karen had brought tears to her eyes, telling her to take as much time as she needed, and giving her the contact information of a substitute teacher Tess knew to be excellent.

She pulled on the rest of her clothes and stood up. He waved at her weakly from the floor but did not attempt to stand. "I like that your mother is staying here. We can see each other whenever we want."

Tess grimaced slightly. Rachel had taken the children into the city that day, and she knew they would return with hundreds of dollars' worth of merchandise from Gap Kids or Crewcuts. Tess couldn't stand the waste. The children had all they needed already, and Rachel's spending scared her. She needed to save her money, as Tess had suggested on more than one occasion. But Rachel would always justify her purchases by saying they were on sale or that Sammy or Rosie didn't have whatever cut of jeans was the latest thing for six-year-olds.

Guy said suggestively, "I have just a little more to do on this project I'm working on. It should be an easy week."

Tess smiled. "I'll call you tomorrow."

She walked home along Henry Street, which was mostly extra wide brownstones belonging to the extremely wealthy or those lucky enough to buy before the neighborhood went real-estate crazy. The cool air helped clear her woozy head.

She had never smoked pot with Patrick, but one of the things she found out during the divorce was that he used to go to the apartment of a friend—a girl with red hair and yellow teeth whom Tess had always pretended not to think was rather stupid—and smoke with her. Tess had wondered what else they did but Molly, who had met the woman at gatherings on more than one occasion, dismissed the notion with a wave of her hand. Tess smiled, remembering her friend's words.

"Tess, she's like the town bicycle. Everyone gets a ride. Why would Patrick, of all people, be any different?"

At home, the apartment was tidy and welcoming, thanks to Tess's mother. The children were glued to the TV, and Rachel sat at the corner of the sectional closest to it, but with her back to the set and her head propped up on a pillow, fast asleep. On the floor at her feet was the predictable mound of clothing purchases for the children.

Tess sighed and walked to the kitchen to get a glass of ice water. Her throat felt jagged from smoking. On the way she passed the dining room table, which was laid out with several paper-bag puppets with goggle eyes and yarn hair, and some other props Tess couldn't quite make out, one of which she thought might be a frog. There was a pile of loose leaf with both children's handwriting, which she knew meant they had written one of their scripts for a puppet show.

Carrying her glass, she kissed her children before going to her room, where she put her feet up on a mound of pillows on her bed, and flipped on her own TV. A rerun of *Law & Order* came on, and she let it drone on in the background, just wanting the noise as company while she rested.

She wiggled her toes and let her head slide back into the pillows, feeling relaxed and thoughtful. Guy was right. Patrick had been such an asshole! What the hell was the matter with her? She told herself that it was because her children were suffering and that was so hard! That explained why she felt as conflicted as she did. But images of Patrick looking kind and sympathetic - that look on his face that made her want to put her arms around him and tell him that everything was going to be okay, even when she didn't fully comprehend what was the matter - shuffled through her mind.

Then there were memories from when they'd first got together— when she'd cried and told him she was pregnant, and he'd knelt in front of her and taken her hand and said it was okay, he was glad. He wanted a baby. She remembered when she'd dreaded telling him she'd accidentally thrown an envelope containing two hundred dollars in cash down the trash chute and he'd immediately said, "Don't worry about it." She recalled a friend telling her how he had spoken about her with pride.

She couldn't comprehend it, couldn't put it together. How was it possible that all that time he was pretending to be her friend and partner he was actually undermining her happiness, knowing what he was doing to her and not caring? Impossible for a mere mortal to understand such depths of illness! She would never fully understand, she knew, and she decided that if, in general, a sociopath sets their eyes on you, forget it. You'll never know. Silently, she vowed to hire a private detective when her own children decided to get married.

Her eye caught a note in her mother's hand, scrawled on an open page of a notebook on her desk. She got up and reached for it, bringing it back to bed with her, and flipping on the lamp next to her bed so she could read it.

Hospital called. Patrick being transferred to palliative tomorrow. Not look good. Doctor suggested bringing children by in morning while P. still communicative.

Tess stared from the note to her door and shook her head in amazement. Her mother really was a pillar of strength. She had managed to take a call like that and still take the kids shopping and supervise a puppet show production without calling or texting her. She hadn't wanted to disturb Tess's afternoon with Guy.

She felt a swell of gratitude followed by a stab of guilt. She sat down on the bed for a moment, trying to let the knowledge that it was probably only a matter of weeks before Patrick died download into her consciousness. He wouldn't be in this world anymore. She would never see him again. She would never hear him say, "I'm sorry."

She clenched the notebook in both hands and shook it.

"If you were dying, he wouldn't give a *shit*," she whispered to herself. "He wouldn't shed a tear. He would celebrate! What the fuck is the matter with you, Tess Shapiro?"

CHAPTER 21

The children were gathering their things for the puppet show and putting them in a plastic bag for her to bring with them to the hospital.

Sammy said, "We need a sheet!"

Rosie added, "And some string and clothes pegs!"

Tess said, "I'll get everything. You guys just get yourselves ready to go."

She grabbed a handful of wooden clothes pegs that she kept in a bowl on the kitchen window sill for sealing opened bags of food, and shoved them into a cloth shopping bag. From the bottom drawer she grabbed a spool of twine and a pair of scissors and tossed them in, then headed to the hall closet where she kept old sheets suitable only for play or beach excursions, folded on a shelf above the coats.

Watching her fold up the sheet so it would fit in the bag, Rosie looked suddenly distraught. "Where will we hang the other side? There was only one chair in Daddy's hospital room when we visited."

"Don't worry," Tess assured her. "We can easily find a second chair."

She put the packed up bag on a chair in the dining room before going to get her own coat and shoes. Rachel was in the kitchen now, unloading the dishwasher.

Tess said, "Mom, just take a break when we're gone, okay? You need to rest!"

Rachel shrugged and raised her palms. "Okay, so I'll rest. Are you bringing the children home afterward or taking them to school?"

Rosie looked up sharply from the dining room, where she was packing up the rest of the puppet-show paraphernalia, to hear the answer. Tess winked at her knowingly.

"School," she said. "I think it will be good for them to see their friends."

Rachel nodded.

When they arrived at the hospital, the nurse behind the reception desk flushed with surprise. "Mr. Faygel has already been moved to palliative."

Tess didn't even try and repress the anger that welled up inside of her. "They promised they'd wait until the afternoon!"

The woman gulped, her glance taking in the deflating expressions on Sammy and Rosie's faces. Even standing a few feet behind Tess, they could tell something was wrong.

Her face now crimson, the nurse said, "I'm so sorry!"

Tess sighed. She tried to calm herself. It wasn't this woman's fault. "Where is he?"

The nurse gave her directions. As it turned out, it wasn't far. Tess turned to Sammy and Rosie.

"Listen," she said. "It looks like Daddy was moved to a different hospital, a nicer one. We have to get back in the car, okay? We're going to go see him there now."

They nodded mutely, but their expressions contained pulses of fear. Tess's heart squeezed in on itself as she led them to the elevators.

The facility they had moved Patrick to reminded Tess of the old-age home in Vancouver in which her grandparents and great-grandparents had ended their days. Although much like a hospital, it at least had a communal dining hall and activities for patients who could make it, comfortable furniture in the rooms, and a brigade of workers constantly swooping down to refill water bottles, attend to IVs, and take vitals.

The view was bright but not spectacular. A cluster of bushes framed the window of Patrick's ground-floor room, which faced a concrete courtyard embellished with beds of lifeless shrubs and spaces for flowers. Tess tried in vain to imagine them filled with blooming floras in the spring.

Sammy and Rosie got to work setting up the puppet show, stringing the sheet between two chairs and hunching behind it. Tess paid only half-attention to the story line, which was about a girl who went to a store and a park, but couldn't find her crocodile. Finally the girl realized it was in her friend's stomach, which allowed Sammy to devour Rosie's puppet with his own, a conclusion that Tess knew Sammy probably conceived of before writing the rest of the story.

Patrick laughed weakly and gestured for the children to come to his bed so he could hug them. Tess had brought bagels and muffins, but Patrick wasn't allowed solids. The children nibbled them instead and then said good-bye, promising to come back the next day.

They drove home in silence, Tess stealing glances in the rear-view mirror to see their expressions. A mixture of sadness and fulfillment—for the successful reception they got for the puppet show, she thought—ebbed between them as they stared out the windows, their profiles turning to black as they entered the tunnel.

They emerged and the car filled with the light of an overcast day. On impulse, Tess turned into the McDonald's drive-through without telling them, and watched in the rearview mirror as they exchanged excited glances. She ordered two Happy Meals from the round speaker in the center of the giant Plexiglas-covered menu.

"Thank you!" they chorused, as Tess took the bags from the girl behind the window and passed them back. Eagerly, they opened them up to fish out their prizes first: plastic *minions* from the movie they'd recently seen. Both had finished eating before Tess pulled up in front of their school.

"Don't forget to go to the office first and get late slips!" she called after them.

"We know!"

The day was gray and still and Tess sat there for a moment, staring at the shiny red paint of the doors that had just closed behind her children. She felt a wave of sickening depression and was loath to just go home. She called Karen and asked if she could swing by the school for a visit.

"The children will be thrilled," her supervisor said. "Just so you know, we just told them that you had some family issues you needed to attend to. No details."

"Got it, thank you, Karen!"

"See you soon!"

The fifth graders gushed with pleasure when they saw her.

"Ms. Shapiro!" they cried, when she appeared at the door.

The substitute, Magda, was a pretty African American woman whose hair fanned out in corkscrew tendrils around her shoulders. When she smiled, her whole face lit up and Tess felt a wash of relief.

They're in good hands, she thought gratefully.

While the children worked, Tess went over the plans with Magda and instructed her about some of the children's special needs. After she left she didn't know what to do, so she walked across the street to Brooklyn Bread, a neighborhood coffee shop where she often ate lunch. Before she walked in, she texted Guy and asked if he wanted to meet for coffee.

I'm in the city today! He texted back. *I wish I could.*

Tess frowned and tried Molly.

Ugh, I'm right in the middle of a shoot. Can we do tomorrow morning?

Tess texted back, *Maybe…have to speak to doctors this afternoon, then will have better idea.*

As she went through the glass doors, Tess realized that it was already afternoon and she hadn't eaten lunch. Still, she didn't feel hungry and just ordered a hazelnut coffee and two pieces of strawberry rugelach from the girl behind the counter. She placed them on one of the small, round Formica tables before sitting down on a red vinyl bench far enough from the door so she wouldn't catch a chill when it opened. Not far from her, a few old-time regulars sipped coffee from paper cups and shared oversized cookies, exchanging gossip that belonged to decades past. Tess took a few sips of the coffee to warm herself before calling Dr. Friedman's number.

By the time she managed to get him on the line, her pastries had been devoured and she dotted at the crumbs with her index finger absently, before sucking on it. Finally, the now familiar voice greeted her, sounding as usual like he had just grabbed the receiver in mid-task and was in a hurry. He didn't answer her questions immediately, but was silent for an ominous moment. Tess imagined him clenching his jaw as he searched for words.

Finally he said, "Look, I'm so sorry, but things are going downhill faster than we anticipated. I think you'll regret it if you don't bring the children in every day. Why don't you bring them in the mornings and take them to school in the afternoons? He's better at that time of day. Then, toward the end, we can make arrangements for you all to sleep here if you'd like. We've done it before."

Tess swallowed hard and tried to think clearly, but she couldn't. A steady wail of sirens going down Court Street made it impossible to decide.

"I'll definitely bring them every morning as you suggested. I'll have to think about the sleeping over. I can't decide about that right now, but I'm glad to hear it's an option."

"No problem. I should see you tomorrow. I'm making my rounds there at around ten."

"Okay, thank you, Doctor." Then she remembered. "Dr. Friedman?"

Thankfully, he was still on the line. "Yes?"

"My husband's family is coming down. They're probably going to be there most of the time. Could you tell them that I will be there with the children in the morning from nine to eleven, and if they could fit their schedule around that, I'd really appreciate it?"

"Meaning you don't want to be there at the same time?"

"Correct."

He sighed. "I'll pass your message along." Then he added, "Ms. Shapiro? Please just consider that the children might want to spend some time with your ex-husband together with his family. We have a lounge and a cafeteria if you want to make yourself scarce."

Tess chewed her lip. "Thank you. I'll think about what you said."

She hung up the phone and looked around her. The old timers were drifting to the glass front of the coffee shop like movie-caricature yokels tentatively approaching an alien from a spaceship that had landed on their farm.

Tess felt vaguely irritated as she looked from them to the street, where more police cars were screaming by, and then to the television set mounted on the corner above the pastry-display counter.

"Turn it up," an elderly man called to the girl behind the counter.

She pointed a remote control in the direction of the T.V. and a row of green volume bars appeared at the bottom and increased in number. Tess strained to hear, but it was difficult to piece together what was happening, beyond some terrible incident in lower Manhattan involving a shooting and a police manhunt.

Tess took out her phone and opened Google News. There she read that a young French reporter named Crafen Roux, who wrote for a locally published French periodical called *French New York*, had been murdered by a drive-by shooter as he entered his midtown office building. His offence, apparently, had been publishing an article not only criticizing, but also satirizing the terrorist group NAFKA.

Camera crews zoomed in on the cordoned-off area where the attack had taken place, though ambulances and police cars obscured any possible view of the entrance-way of the building.

She looked up again to the TV, now showing security-camera footage of a black car pulling up to the front of the building, and then its driver shooting a slight man in tan pants and blue shirt in the back. He surged upward with the impact, before collapsing on the sidewalk in a pool of his own blood seconds before the car sped away.

Beneath the grotesque image flashed a crawler that said, "Warning, footage may be too graphic for some viewers."

Tess stared for several moments, blinking, but the only thought making it around and around her dazed brain was, *Crafen!* That's not a name.

CHAPTER 22

Tess texted her mother and told her to look at the news.

Rachel texted back, *I saw. Unbelievable!*

She watched the set for a few more minutes, transfixed, then shook her head to break the spell. She tried to turn her mind to practical matters. The children would be getting out of school soon. There didn't seem to be any point in driving the car the six blocks back home before going to get them. By the time she got home, it would almost be time to go back.

Instead, she got up and walked slowly towards the door, her thoughts strayed to a place she could not see. The sudden pain of her forehead smacking into the glass door ultimately shook her awake.

"I'm fine!" she assured the fellow patrons who were uttering exclamations of sympathy and asking if she was alright.

Rubbing her forehead with a gloved hand and feeling both annoyed and foolish, Tess walked at a sharp clip towards PS 30, where a crowd of parents was already gathered in the schoolyard to wait for dismissal. They stood in clusters with their arms folded, indignant expressions on their faces as they spoke about the terrorist incident.

Tess did not join them but instead sat on a bench, catching snippets of conversation from around her.

"Great," one mother was saying, her breath coming out in visible white clouds as she pushed a stroller back and forth with unnecessary vigor. "Now they're coming here."

Her remarks were met with angry shakes of the head and mumbles of agreement.

"Germany needs to do something about this. It's their responsibility," grumbled a stay-at-home dad Tess had known since Sammy and his daughter were in preschool together. As he spoke, his black-framed glasses steamed up under his pilled brown woolen hat.

When the children came out, Tess strode over to them and took them by the hands, steering them purposefully out of the schoolyard.

"We want to stay and play," Sammy complained.

"It's too cold," Tess said absently, tugging them along.

In truth, she didn't feel like being a part of the toxic conversations around her. Something pricked at her mind, and she felt a desperate need to be alone and think it through.

As soon as they got inside the front door of their apartment, Sammy and Rosie dove to Rachel's sides to cuddle with her while she stared at the television footage of the attack.

"What's that about, Grandma?" Rosie asked.

Rachel shook her head and reached for the remote to shut off the set when Tess said, "Don't!"

She perched on the end of the sofa and stared at the set. The crawler summarized: "French reporter Crafen Roux shot dead by terrorists. NAFKA claims responsibility."

Tess picked up the remote, ready to shut it off if the gruesome footage of the actual shooting came back on, but for now it was just a reporter regurgitating the details of the story. Behind him people gathered, hoisting black signs on which were printed in white letters: I AM CRAFEN. The reporter acknowledged them with a backward jab of his thumb, calling them "a mark of solidarity" and "an affirmation of the American commitment to freedom of the press."

Tess stared at the screen pensively. Then it came to her.

"It's an anagram."

Her mother pulled back her head and peered at her, perplexed.

"What's an *ag-ro-nam*?" Sammy asked.

Tess did not look at them. "Crafen. It's an anagram for France." She strode over to her desk and grabbed a pen and a piece of paper from the printer. When she came back she wrote in uppercase letters: C-R-A-F-E-N.

And then, beneath that: F-R-A-N-C-E. Then she drew lines to connect each letter in the name to the word *France*.

The realization sent shockwaves through her, but her mother merely shrugged and said, "That's interesting."

Tess looked her in amazement. "Just interesting?"

"Well, yes. I mean what else would you call it?"

Tess sputtered, "I don't know, but it's more than just interesting."

Her mother continued to look at her, confused.

Tess explained. "Crafen isn't a name!"

"Well, how would you know, dear? It's French."

Tess shook her head, exasperated. "Mom, you're the one that sent me to Switzerland for a year to learn French. There's no such name as Crafen."

Her mother dipped her chin and looked at her evenly. "Tess, I don't think that in the period of one year you heard every French name ever invented. Besides, if it's a French name, as in *from France*, you might not have heard it in Switzerland."

Tess swallowed. Something hard and hot was melting in her brain. "I have to go somewhere. I'll be back in an hour or so."

She headed to the front door.

"Where dear? Where are you going?"

Rosie said, "Mommy?"

Tess bit her lip and hesitated, seeing the alarm in her daughter's eyes. She took a deep breath and forced a smile.

"I'm going to get us some ingredients to make dessert. It's been a hard day. How about we make cookies?"

The children chorused their enthusiasm and Tess smiled.

"Be back soon!"

She closed the door behind her and pushed away any feelings of guilt as she plunged down the fire stairs and out onto the sidewalk.

Tess walked the seven blocks to Guy's house in long, quick strides. Despite the cold, perspiration broke out on her forehead, and she swiped at it with the back of her gloved hand and pulled off her hat, shoving it in her purse. She had no idea what she was going to do when she got there. What if Yves was home?

But by some incredibly fortunate coincidence, she saw them walking together up the street, carrying bags of groceries, at the same time she reached their block.

"Well, hello!" she said, in her most cheerful teacher voice.

Guy looked at her sideways. "Ms. Shapiro! How pleasant to see you here!"

Yves gazed at her silently, his eyes filled with pleasure and surprise. Tess smiled at him. "Hello, Yves!"

She took a deep breath and addressed Guy. "I guess you saw the news today. Terrible, isn't it?"

Guy nodded. "Yes, I was just explaining it to Yves. He is nervous, but I explained there is nothing to worry about."

Tess nodded. "Nothing to worry about," she repeated, almost to herself.

Guy squinted and looked at her sideways. "Something is the matter, Ms. Shapiro?"

Tess perked up and looked at him squarely. "Actually, I'm glad I ran into you. I wanted to ask you something."

Guy raised his eyebrows and waited.

Tess said, "Is Crafen a name?"

Guy pulled his head back and said something to Yves in French, handing him a ring of keys from his pocket. Yves nodded and scurried ahead to their house, where he let himself in as the two adults watched. Then Guy turned to her.

"Tess, what is the matter? You look very strange. Is something wrong? Did your ex-husband die?"

Tess looked at him sharply. "What? No!"

"You look unwell. Do you want to sit on the stair?" He took her elbow and indicated the bottom stair of the brownstone they were standing in front of.

Tess pulled her arm away. "No," she repeated, more forcefully. Then, seeing Guy's face, she realized how out of it she must seem. She took a deep breath.

"I just want to know. Is Crafen a name? Because I've never heard it before."

Guy set his groceries down and opened his palms. "Of course it is a name. It is a French name. It is not so common, but I have known a few people with this name."

Tess felt as though she'd just woken up on the train only to discover she'd missed her stop. She struggled to keep her expression even, as she lowered herself onto the bottom stair after all.

"It's just…it's an anagram, for France. Crafen is an anagram for France."

Guy shrugged his shoulders and lifted his palms again. He spoke to her as if pointing out something obvious to an imbecile. "Yes, that is why it is a French name. It is a patriotic name."

Now Tess felt a wash of heated embarrassment. Of course. Of course it was. That's why she never heard it in Switzerland. It wasn't an anagram for Switzerland!

Guy stood up suddenly. "Listen, I have to go inside or Yves will be worried."

He seemed reluctant to leave her, so she did her best to reassure him.

"Yes, yes. I'm fine. It was just the shock of seeing Patrick," she lied. "I—they switched him into palliative care. He's going downhill fast. It's only a matter of weeks now. And his family is coming. I just—I don't know. Nothing like this has ever happened to me before."

She meant the turn of mind, but Guy assumed she was still speaking of Patrick's dying. He said reasonably, "I understand. I had to deal with my parents' deaths and my wife's. The first time you have to deal with death is very difficult."

Tess nodded. She didn't bother to point out that she'd already had to deal with her father's death. She was grateful Guy had come up with a satisfactory explanation of her behavior for himself. He leaned over and patted her knee before leaving her and she walked home slowly, feeling foolish and sick.

It wasn't until she reached the front door of her building that she realized she'd forgotten both to drive back the car and to buy the promised ingredients for cookies. The car could stay where it was, she told herself, and she turned and hurried across the street to the store, mentally compiling a list which included chocolate chips, butter, eggs and flour.

CHAPTER 23

I nevitably, she saw *them* again.

Tess watched as Patrick raised his eyes to the door and said "hi" in a croaky voice. Then the children rushed to the door. She didn't need to turn around.

"Grannie!" They cried.

Reluctantly, Tess turned to watch as her children then hugged and greeted Patrick's sister and brother-in-law.

Feeling the disdain rise inside of her, Tess shuddered and turned away. For the first time, she didn't feel any inclination to reserve judgment or keep an open mind. They were frosty-haired, loudly attired, narrow-minded hicks. They were what Europeans laughed about when they spoke of Americans. And they were anti-Semites to the core.

But Virginia tapped her arm so that she turned and allowed herself to be greeted through piles of pink lipstick.

"Hello, Tess, I hope you are well."

Tess just raised her eyebrows. *Sure you do.* But looking at her children's happy faces, she realized the truth of Dr. Friedman's advice.

She said, "I'll leave you guys alone for a while with the children. Please bring them to me in the lounge in half an hour. I'm going to take them to school for the afternoon, and they have to eat lunch first."

"That's fine," Virginia replied.

Tess explained to the children that they were going to stay for an extra while and took herself to the cafeteria, where she purchased a cup of hot tea, and then to the gift shop, where she bought a fashion magazine for something to occupy her time.

She hadn't looked at a fashion magazine for years but now, flipping through the glossy pages, she remembered how in her earliest sketches of Andrea Chambers she had worn fashions copied straight out of the pages of British *Vogue* and *Elle*. These, she recalled nostalgically, were acquired on Sunday jaunts to Oakridge Drugs, one of the few places in Vancouver that were open on that day of the week.

Generally, she left with both a magazine and either a large package of strawberry Twizzlers or a box of Cadbury's butterscotch, which she would later suck on slowly as she lay on the shag carpet of her basement room, projecting her future onto the stills of elegantly dressed models in exotic locations. Peering at the images now, Tess found it hard to believe. Now they looked to her like babies playing dress-up. The images did not move or even interest her.

Patick's sister emerged with the children twenty minutes later, as Tess had requested. While more thickly set than she had been when Tess first met her over a decade earlier, Lorraine remained otherwise unchanged. Dark-blond hair hung in greasy-looking lanks to beneath her shoulders, and she still wore the same blue eyeshadow and clumpy black mascara that Tess remembered. She looked, however, smiling and indulgent as she led the children toward Tess.

"I'm glad we got a chance to see them," she said brightly.

Tess nodded. She felt her resolve soften, and she realized she had been selfish. "Well, if you'd like to do it again tomorrow, we can make the same arrangement."

Lorraine smiled. "We'd like that, wouldn't we, guys?"

She looked to Sammy and Rosie, who nodded eagerly.

Tess said, "I'll wait out here while you visit together. You don't need to stay away in the mornings. It's okay."

Lorraine started to cry. She raised her palms to cover her eyes and sobbed into them. Tess didn't know what to do, so she stood up and hugged Lorraine stiffly, patting her back.

"I'm so sorry," she said.

She felt Lorraine nod. After a moment she seemed to compose herself and pulled away, taking a deep, tremulous breath while wiping at the smears of black makeup that had pooled under her eyes. She blew her nose and offered a self-deprecating smile to the children.

"Okay, so we'll see you tomorrow, okay?"

She tried to keep her voice bright, but it broke on the last word and the children noticed. They looked at her with concern.

"Okay," they said quietly.

And Tess looked at them sympathetically, berating herself for the feelings of envy that accompanied the realization that her children would always belong—at least partially—to Patrick's family.

Patrick was getting weaker with each passing day, and with each passing day Tess was becoming more and more depressed. She couldn't understand it, and neither could Guy.

In exasperation, he suggested, "Maybe you still love him!"

They were sitting at a small round table at Café Reggio in the West Village, having just seen a spy thriller at the Angelica Theater. The tiny space reminded Tess of the house Guy had rented, with its oil paintings, tin ceiling, and turn-of-the-last-century feel. Tess stared at the untouched piece of cheesecake in front of her and sipped at a cup of black tea, served to her in an overly ornate pink tea cup with a matching saucer. At his words, she looked up sharply and recoiled.

"No," she said. "I don't. I can't even think about…*being* with him again that way. It makes me sick."

Guy chewed at the corner of his lip, his arms folded across his chest. He looked unconvinced.

"There is some lingering feelings," he insisted.

Tess shook her head and sighed. "I wish you would stop saying that. It's not true. I feel resentful and mournful for my lost opportunity for a happy family. I mourn for what was done to me; what was taken from me and can never be returned."

"*Bon*, okay," Guy conceded, and motioned for the waitress to bring the check with an air of irritation.

Tess glared at him, her anger rising.

"You don't believe me," she said through clenched teeth.

Guy shrugged. He attempted to put on a sympathetic face. "I think you should go to see a therapist. You need to sort these things out."

Tess felt another flash of anger and was about to lash out at him for being so unsympathetic, when it occurred to her that he might be right. She did feel like she was coming unhinged, a bit. Something was tearing her apart, and she herself didn't even know what it was. Perhaps therapy was a good idea. It had been a lifesaver during the divorce, although that therapist didn't take insurance and was pretty expensive. Molly still saw someone—swore by her and said she took every kind of insurance. Maybe after the Thanksgiving weekend…Ribbons of thought curled and unfurled in her mind.

Finally she frowned and looked at Guy. "I'll think about it."

They rode the subway home in silence, Tess feeling confused and awful. Guy got off at his stop first, kissing her lightly before he departed. "Everything will be better, you will see."

She smiled weakly and watched him depart, feeling like she'd inadvertently knocked over a precious china cup with her elbow.

Thanksgiving was a comforting day. Even though both Tess and her mother were Canadian, where Thanksgiving came in October and was generally not celebrated by Jews, they did their best to cook the traditional meal that the children were used to, her mother electing to buy the turkey breast only, rather than the whole bird. This she smothered in a delectable garlic-and-honey-mustard marinade that filled the apartment with delicious roasting smells. Tess let the children dot the sweet-potato casserole with miniature marshmallows before she put it in the oven, and she herself did the green beans with almonds and tossed a salad with creamy balsamic vinaigrette.

As they sat around the table, Tess knew it felt right, like a family. They skipped the part about being thankful, Tess thinking it would stir feelings about Patrick. Instead she said, "Dig in!" with as much gusto as she could muster.

Afterward Sammy cried, "I'm too full for dessert!"

His eyes filled with regret, and he looked like he was about to cry. Tess smiled indulgently and smothered him with kisses.

"We can have dessert later," she said, ruffling his hair. "Do you guys want to play a little bit first?"

Rosie agreed, and Tess and her mother did the dishes while the children put together an elaborate Lego structure in the living room.

Tess fell asleep on the sofa, and her mother only woke her when it was time to put the children to sleep.

"You missed dessert," she said.

Tess blinked and looked around her, startled. "How long was I asleep?" she asked.

"Two hours. You looked like you needed it," her mother said, patting her shoulder after she sat up, blinking and stretching.

Tess sighed. "I did."

Later that night she sat in bed sketching, her mind a swirl of thoughts that needed to work themselves out in their usual way.

PANEL ONE

Young men and women dressed in army fatigues jog up a hill. Among them is a young Andrea. A younger, brown-haired version of Sergeant Anton is barking at them:

"And now everyone has to go up and down this hill six times because Andrea did not clean her rifle properly this morning."

Andrea is visibly red in the face as her fellow troopers admonish her: "When will you ever learn?" and "This is the second group punishment we've had to do because of *you*, Andrea! Why are you such a screwup?"

A thought bubble attached to Andrea says, "But it's not true! My rifle was clean and my bunk was made properly! When will these idiots realize that the whole point of collective punishment is to get us to work together?"

PANEL TWO

Anton regards Andrea through slit eyes underneath his sergeant's hat. Andrea turns at the bottom of the hill and grunts. A thought bubble emanating from her proclaims: "This is it! I'm finishing with this hill and then I'm handing in my rifle! I QUIT!"

PANEL THREE

The troopers are taking off their hats and wiping their brows, heading toward a low wooden building with a sign that says "Mess Hall." Andrea remains standing at attention in front of Anton, however, with her rifle still on her back and her hat on.

She says, "May I speak with you privately, please?"

Anton squints at her. "What do you want?

PANEL FOUR

Andrea flushes as she speaks. "Um, I'd like to say that I'm thankful for this learning opportunity, but I don't think it's quite the right thing for me so I'd—uh—like to quit, go home."

Anton's face is inscrutable as he regards her. "Come with me."

PANEL FIVE

The pair is seen from behind, walking to a bunker. The thought bubble emanating from Andrea's head says, "Thank goodness! He probably just needs me to sign some paperwork, and then I can get out of here. I'll need to call the airport, of course, and let my mother know I'm coming..."

PANEL SIX
Andrea and Anton sit across from one another, on either side of a metal desk in a small dark room. Above them, a domed metal light with a single bulb casts a yellow circle onto a table covered in piles of paperwork. Anton sits with his elbows on the arms of his chair, his index fingers lightly touching his lips. Andrea leans forward and speaks.

"So do you need me to sign something? I'm sorry, I'm not sure how this works. Is there some paperwork I need to fill out?"

Anton says simply, "I have been watching you. I think you might be right for a special mission."

PANEL SEVEN
Andrea looks at him perplexedly. "Mission? What are you talking about? I said I want to quit!"

Anton continues, "I believe you are a young woman of particular intelligence and insight. I am offering you an opportunity to experience adventure and excitement for the rest of your life. If you say yes, you will be rich and independent from this day forward."

PANEL EIGHT
Andrea gasps, "You want me to be a spy?"

Anton pushes some paperwork and a pen forward. "Sign here and you won't regret it. Then I can tell you about your first mission."

PANEL NINE
In a shaking hand, Andrea signs. But the thought bubble above her says, "What am I doing? I must be insane!"

PANEL TEN

Andrea pushes the contract back and says, "I'm listening."

Anton nods and smiles. "*Bon,* first let me ask you. Do you speak German?"

PANEL ELEVEN

"No," Andrea says. "Why would you think I spoke German?"

Anton looks disappointed. He furrows his brow and says, "It's just that it is similar to Yiddish. Do you speak this?"

PANELS TWELVE THROUGH THIRTEEN

Tess looks at him in astonishment. "Nobody speaks Yiddish any-more! And why do you need people who speak German?"

Anton leans toward her. "Andrea, you may not realize this, but we have problems in this country. Four peoples, with four lan-guages, living under one flag in such a tiny country…it is not very sustainable."

Andrea shrugs. "It seems to be working okay."

Anton shakes his head. "Look, your people know the kinds of problems Germans cause. They are always planning on how they will fulfill their destiny: The Master Race. So, we have the same problem here."

PANELS FOURTEEN THROUGH FIFTEEN

Andrea looks surprised, "You do?"

Anton nods vigorously. "Oh, yes! It may not be as outward as your people have experienced, you understand, but they cause difficulties in subtle ways that make it impossible to get anything worthwhile done. It is to undermine the Swiss government, so they can show how ineffectual French and Italian peoples are compared to Germans."

Andrea cocks her head. "I had no idea."

Anton frowns and nods. "Yes, this is the problem, you see? It is always subtle, always sneaky, so we have no way to defeat them. But if there were an outward battle, there is no way the Germans would win. The French and Italian Swiss would overpower them. We could remove the German presence from our soil!"

PANEL SIXTEEN
Andrea flushes and opens her eyes wide in horror. "Remove them?"

Anton raises his hands. "I do not mean kill them. I mean…assimilate them into either French or Italian culture. Eliminate their presence in government."

PANELS SEVENTEEN THROUGH EIGHTEEN
Andrea still looks shocked as Anton continues.

"So, this is what we need to do. We need to make it an outward battle. Do you understand?"

Andrea nods slowly. "How will you do that?"

Anton says, "Well, do you know the Cathedral St. Nicholas in Fribourg?"

Andrea shakes her head.

Anton says, "Ah, no? It is *magnifique*. You must see it soon, because the Germans are going to blow it up."

Andrea gasps, "You know this?"

PANEL NINETEEN (SMALL CIRCLE BETWEEN PANELS. CLOSE-UP OF ANTON.)
Anton rubs one eyelid with his index finger.

"Do you not understand, Andrea?"

PANEL TWENTY
Andrea's eyes open wide. "You mean, we…?"

Anton nods. "You will need to dress in a German style and speak a little German. Make your presence known in the town. Don't worry, we will train you."

PANEL TWENTY-ONE (CIRCLE BETWEEN PANELS. CLOSE-UP OF ANDREA.)
"I…I can't do that. Anyway, I don't look German!"

PANEL TWENTY-TWO
Anton holds up the contract. "I told you we will take care of these details. Anyway, this is your first assignment. You will fulfill it as ordered."

By the time Tess finished she was exhausted, but she still took time to look over her work, wondering at her own imaginings and what they meant.

She shook her head. The world seemed to be turning itself upside down for her so she could look at the engine and see how it really worked, but she couldn't get it, couldn't understand. Grunting, she slid out of bed and grabbed the stapler off her desk to crunch the pages together, before depositing them in her chest.

Then, on impulse, she went out to the living room and grabbed her phone to put on the charger in her room.

It rang in the middle of the night.

CHAPTER 24

Tess stared at Patrick's family's backs, huddled in a rough circle on the green vinyl chairs in the reception room. A man with a clerical collar held two sets of hands. As she neared, she only heard him say, "In Jesus' name, Amen."

"Amen," they chorused.

Tess stood nearby, not wanting to intrude, waiting for them to notice her.

Her brother-in-law, Jeff, spotted her first and came over. Short, with thick eyebrows and dark spiky hair, he shook her hand warmly and thanked her for coming.

Tess said, "Were you all here when…he passed?"

Jeff dipped his chin. He spoke in a quiet voice. "We were sleeping in chairs in Patrick's room. We heard the machines go off, then the doctors and nurses ran in, but he was already gone."

Jeff's hands were buried deep in his jeans pockets. He looked at the floor. Tess tried to imagine the scene and wondered what she would have felt if she had been there. She glanced behind Jeff at Lorraine and Virginia, who were weeping and comforting one another. Tess caught her breath. Witnessing the depths of their grief, she felt guilty for her uncharitable thoughts of a few days before.

Jeff inclined his head in the direction of his family and said, "I'll be right back."

Tess nodded and stared after him. Prior to meeting Patrick's family, she had had no notion of Christianity whatsoever—not even the basics beyond Jesus, cross, Easter, and Christmas. It was upon gleaning the intensity of their discomfort about her religious background that compelled her to finally pick up a copy of the New Testament in a hotel room on their way down to visit them one Christmas. She had slogged through the wordy prose while Patrick got some work done on his laptop that first day, and even took it with her to continue reading in the car on the second day of their journey. Patrick said it was okay; they wanted you to take it.

She remembered being amazed by the derogatory image of Jews in the Christian bible. It felt, to her, laced with genuine disgust and hatred. She thought, any modern attempts to recant this or reinterpret it so that it is fit for modern ears is meaningless. It's here. It's right here.

Whereas the bible of her youth contained no mention of the Christians whatsoever, theirs was based on a negative reaction to her people's existence. And Patrick's family members were God-fearing, church-going Christians, no doubt about it. No wonder they were glad to see the back of her!

She shook off the negative thoughts as Jeff appeared again.

"Where is he now?" She asked.

Jeff grimaced. "They took him away. We have to make funeral arrangements from here, and they'll arrange for the transport of the body to and from the airport."

Tess shivered involuntarily. "When will the funeral be?"

In the Jewish religion, funerals had to be the day after the person died, but she had no idea what the custom was in the Christian religion.

Jeff shrugged. "They'll let us know, I guess." He read the confused look on her face. "It'll be within the next week or so. I'll let you know and make sure you get a copy of the death certificate. You know, for the flights."

Jeff, she knew, was always economizing. But she was glad of this detail. She didn't feel like spending thousands of dollars on flights and a hotel for Patrick's funeral.

She indicated with her chin to where Lorraine and Virginia sat clinging to one another, attempting to restrain their bursts of anguished sobs. "Should I go say something to them?"

Jeff screwed his bottom lip around and bit it before releasing it again. "Maybe not," he said. "I'll tell them you stopped by."

"Thank you, Jeff," she said sincerely.

The funeral was a three-part ordeal. First there was the viewing. Tess had never been to one of these. It took place on a cold evening, in a single-story stucco building in the smoky Blue Mountains. Inside were two main rooms, carpeted in blue, with shimmery white wallpaper intersected with yellow stripes at regular intervals. The rooms were separated by a narrower space, in which Tess now stood, holding her children by the hands and looking at the shellacked wooden casket, up to which relatives walked reverently, mumbled, and walked away from crying.

Then they went to sit on metal folding chairs nearby or went to the front room, where store-bought platters of cubed yellow and white cheese and Town crackers, or sorted circles of carrot and celery sticks pointing at a bowl of lumpy white dip, sat on a folded out table next to a pile of napkins and an assortment of canned sodas.

Tess held her children's hands and stared into the room where Patrick lay. She had forgotten how big Patrick's extended family was. She recalled first meeting them at a Fourth of July picnic on a perfect, blue-skied and sunny mountain day. At the time, she had been full of a feeling of acceptance, dismissing any notion that ordinary people bore any negative feelings toward her because of her religious background. In truth, their difference thrilled her to a certain extent, and she opened her mind to understand them. Funnily enough, she thought of her Rabbis as she sought to know them. It was they who had instructed her that the Talmud says: "Everyone has something to teach, and something to learn."

She had even stood in a prayer circle with them, holding hands as they thanked the Lord for the bounty they were about to receive, and said *Ay-men*, instead of *Ah-men* a little too loudly. When she looked up, a cousin—who had gone to college in a big city and had a Jewish room-mate—was looking at her with a humorous twinkle in his eye.

That same cousin approached her now, wearing a gray suit a shade darker than his slicked back hair. He was kind, she remembered, and she took a deep breath.

"Clive!"

They shook hands and Clive embraced her. "I'm real sorry, Tess. Not just about this, but about the divorce and everything. I want you to know that we'll always think of you as family." He nodded in the direction of the children. "Kids too. They're always welcome here."

Hot tears of gratitude sprang to Tess's eyes, and she blinked them away.

"Thank you, Clive. I can tell you really mean that."

"I do, sincerely." He motioned toward the casket. "You never been to one of these before, have you?"

Tess shook her head and gulped. She had never seen a dead body before and wasn't sure she wanted to.

Clive said, "If you like, I can bring the children up. It does them good to have a chance to say good-bye. When they see him, they'll understand that his body is no longer with us, but his soul is gone to heaven to be with God."

Clive looked meaningfully at the children, who were drinking in his every word. Tess felt relieved he'd said "God" and not "Jesus," and wondered if it was on purpose, out of consideration for her. Tess nodded and thanked him, but she knew she had to be brave and bring the children herself.

When Tess saw Patrick's body, she was reminded of all the stories she had read in the New Testament of Jesus going into different towns and villages and curing people who were possessed by demons. Supine on a white satin pillow, his cheeks slack and his arms folded across his chest, Patrick looked like the person she had fallen in love with.

In an instant she knew that that moment, however short lived, had been genuine. She had loved him and, in the corners of his being that weren't sociopathic, he had loved her. It's just that, after a while, the demons had taken over again.

His face became blurry and Tess realized she was crying, but she didn't want to let go of her children's hands to wipe away the tears. They wore tragic looks on their faces as they peered at their father, tears streaming down their cheeks, as well. They spoke no words to one another, but after a few moments, Rosie whispered tremulously, "Good-bye, Daddy," and Tess knew it was time to walk away with them.

She stood by a pillared outgrowth in the wall, nibbling on a carrot stick and taking sips of Coke while the children mingled with their cousins and, finding Virginia, Lorraine and Jeff, embraced them and allowed themselves to be gathered up on their laps.

Her illusions of mutual acceptance that she draped around herself in her twenties now lay at her feet like a fallen curtain, but she also understood that it wasn't everyone who rejected her. Evil, she had come to understand, didn't have a religion, and religions themselves were neither good nor bad. The rabbis had been right, after all. She had leaned great things - important things - from her years trying to understand what was at the core of the faith that permeated these people and this place. Their idea that it was everyone's mission and obligation to love everyone else was apparent from their frequent verbal affirmations.

Whether or not they practiced or believed this was beside the point, Tess now decided. If, despite everything, people could just love and support one another, then every one's dreams would come true. It was a great idea; a beautiful idea, and she would never really have understood it had she not met Patrick. This she knew to be true.

The funeral the next day was held at a small church with wood-paneled walls and velvet-cushioned pews. On a blackboard next to the altar, someone had written the page to turn to in their bible or hymnal—Tess wasn't quite certain—with white chalk. Tess assumed this was from the previous Sunday, since no one had a book in their hand, now. She stood between her children as the congregation sang "Amazing Grace," grateful that the preacher called out the words for each verse before they were to sing them.

Afterward, they drove in a hearse-led procession through the mountain roads to the grave site, Tess driving her maroon Toyota rental behind the limousine with Patrick's mother, sister, and brother-in-law.

She was touched by the cars that pulled over to the side of the road and got out to bow their heads in respect. It reminded her—unnaturally, perhaps—of the Day of Remembrance in Israel, which had occurred during a visit there with her senior class in high school. The sirens wailed and everyone froze, got out of their cars, and stood where they were for a moment of silence to honor the fallen soldiers of past wars.

At the grave site, the preacher spoke about Jesus and love and everlasting life, which Tess only half heard. She was thinking of her own father's funeral, and how it differed from this one. Then, she had used a shovel to heave dirt onto the casket and spoken the mourner's *kaddish* in Hebrew with her mother, which she had taken pains to memorize the night before.

The casket was lowered, and she found herself whispering it to herself with shut eyes: *"Yit'gadal v'yit'kadash sh'mei raba…"* Tess knew the prayer was meant for Jewish people only, but for some reason, she felt that this was why she needed to say it.

CHAPTER 25

Tess was glad to be back at work and to have the children back at school. She had no idea what the future would look like, but in the warm brightness of her classroom, she felt at peace with herself and knew that whatever came next, she could handle it.

She hadn't reached out to Guy yet. She wasn't sure why, but she wanted a few days to let everything settle in her mind. Yves' babysitter picked him up on the first day, and on the second day she thought she should probably text Guy during her lunch hour, since he would have heard of her return.

At eleven o'clock, however, Karen White appeared at her door, looking out of breath and distraught. She waved Tess over. Tess looked at her inquisitively.

"Keep working in your math workbooks," she instructed her class. "If you have a question, you may quietly ask someone at your table."

She walked over to Karen and nodded. "What's up?"

"There's been another terrorist attack. It's the French embassy on the Upper East Side. It's been completely demolished by a bomb. So far twenty-eight people are confirmed dead."

Tess gasped, her heart picking up its pace. "Is it...was it...?"

Karen squeezed her eyes shut momentarily and nodded. "NAFKA? Yes, that's what it sounds like."

Tess shook her head in disbelief. Karen continued in a purposeful, businesslike tone. "Listen, we're in a doubly difficult position here. First of all, we might be a target."

She waved a hand as if to silence a protesting remark, but Tess was all ears. "I know it's a long shot, but the Department of Education wants us to be on lockdown. That means nobody in or out."

Tess nodded. "Got it."

"The other thing is that we're not sure if any of our French families might have been impacted. We have a few students whose parents are diplomats. We have to find out if they're all right before the children find out. So no turning on the computers, and obviously no telling the children."

Tess nodded again, more slowly. "Is there anything else I need to do?"

"We're dismissing from the auditorium, so let the class know. You'll be sitting in the last two rows, on the right side, if your back is to the stage."

Tess assured Karen that she understood and went back to her class, thoughts chasing each other like agitated ghosts in her mind.

At noon she texted Guy to let him know she was back and what was going on. Furtively, she checked her phone every half hour throughout the remainder of the day but by dismissal time, he hadn't written back.

When everyone was assembled in the auditorium, she watched as the parents were ushered in by grade, starting with kindergarten, to pick up their children. Flashbacks of 9/11 filtered through her mind as she watched their faces from in front of the stage. Like that fateful day, their expressions showed shock, horror, and disbelief. As the crowd thinned out, Karen appeared at her side and heaved a sigh of relief.

"Nobody's parents were impacted," she said. "There's a boy in the third grade whose aunt was killed, but that's all. We were able to call everyone."

Tess said, "Which boy?"

Karen told her, and she had a vague recollection of an Alfalfa-looking boy with black hair in a cow's lick and lots of freckles.

When it was just the fifth grade left, Tess's heart began to pound hard. Guy would come, she was sure. She felt embarrassed for the way she had acted before the funeral, and worried that it had impacted his feelings for her. She wanted to show him she was different now. She felt different. But this was neither the time nor the place, she knew. She prepared herself to be professional and teacher-like.

Parents, holding their children by the hand, approached her to exchange a few worried words, shaking their heads and looking cloudy eyed with doomsday premonitions. Tess conversed with them, squeezing hands and giving brief hugs. Then, when they had departed, she looked around her and saw that everyone had left except Yves. He looked panicked and forlorn, sitting in a seat by himself at the back of the room, his head swiveling around to see where his babysitter or father was.

Tess was about to hurry over and reassure him when the door swung open. Guy breezed in and Tess saw with surprise that he had cut his hair. Fashionably suave and European, it gusted over the tops of his ears as he walked. He appeared not to see her as his eyes swept the seats in search of his son. Yves tumbled passed the row of seats toward him and Tess remained very still, watching. For in the forty minutes it had taken for all the children to be picked up, every parent's expression had borne the same look of shock and sadness. But Guy looked perfectly calm. In fact, he looked proud, and like he was repressing laughter for a private joke.

Tess swallowed and opened her mouth, but no words came. She watched them hug, and Guy took Yves by the hand and led him out of the room.

Later, as she walked home down Smith Street with her own children, having explained to them in as simple and nonfrightening terms as possible what had happened, she turned her face to the cold gray December sky as the first snowflakes of the season drifted wetly onto her forehead and cheeks.

"Snow!" Sammy cried.

Tess nodded but did not speak. A knot was uncoiling in her mind, and she knew she had to be very careful not to speak and so disturb it in its intricate workings.

Rosie said, "Mommy, is there going to be a war?"

And the knot undid itself and she knew. She looked down at her daughter who was kicking a stone halfheartedly down the sidewalk as she walked.

Tess took a deep breath and shrugged, smiling weakly.

"I don't know, baby. I really don't know."

CHAPTER 26

The dark bough that stretched across the windows of Tess's living room was covered in snow, and her children were hunched on their knees with their stomachs pressed up against the back of the sofa, staring at the deep white piles that shrouded every car, stoop, and tree.

Tess groaned as she shuffled toward the percolating coffee machine. Why did they always wake up early on weekends, or on days when school was canceled? For had it not been for the mayor declaring a state of emergency on account of the terrorist attack, and ordering all residents to stay in their homes, school would still have been canceled on account of the snow.

Rachel, who had agreed to stay on until after Hanukkah, was thankfully still sleeping. Tess poured herself a giant mug of the caffeinated beverage and topped it off with a generous splash of whole milk.

Sammy said, "Look, Mommy, look at all the snow."

"Mmmm," Tess mumbled, slipping into her usual corner.

"Can we go outside?"

Tess shook her head and pointed at her mug. "Later."

He turned back to take in the scene, and the two of them chatted excitedly, making plans for their excursion to the courtyard later. When the doorbell rang, and she'd only had two sips of coffee, Tess wanted to cry.

"I bet it's Gila and Claude!" Rosie exclaimed, running to the door.

Sure enough, the living room shortly absorbed the siblings from the fourth floor that Sammy and Rosie often played with. From behind them, their mother's voice was tentative but cheerful.

"Are you decent? Can we come in?"

Tess looked down at her polka-dot pajama bottoms and Superman sweatshirt. "I look amazing. Come in. It's a crime to waste this."

Yes, that sounds about right, she thought.

Nathalie had large, smiling, almond-shaped eyes and dark hair streaked with blond. She and her children were dressed in winter clothes—the children wore shiny colorful snow pants—and Nathalie was carrying two disc-shaped sleds.

"I was going to take the kids down to the courtyard before the snow gets all flattened," she said. "I was wondering if you wanted me to take your kids down too."

Tess did, but she groaned inwardly at the prospect of getting them dressed in their snowsuits when she'd just woken up. Not that there was a choice.

"We have the same sleds!" Sammy cried. "They're in my mom's closet. I'm going to get them."

While he pounded down the hall, Tess got up and invited Nathalie to sit while she got the kids ready. Fortunately, Rosie pronounced herself old enough to dress herself.

"Can I get you a coffee?" Tess offered.

From his room, she could hear Sammy fighting with a clothes hanger, trying to get his snowsuit down.

Nathalie shook her head. "Already had it," she said. "These guys woke me up at five. And after yesterday's news, that was all I needed." She rolled her eyes and shook her head.

Tess imitated her, shaking her head and rolling her eyes too. She looked at Nathalie's expression to make sure she got it right.

"I hear that."

Her retort sounded affected and phony to her own ears. "Need to work on that," she thought.

By the time they left, Rachel was up and pouring herself a mug—black, to save the calories. She settled on the sofa opposite Tess and surveyed the scene outside, shaking her head.

"So what are they saying about the attack today?" she asked.

"I don't know. I just got up and it was party city in here."

She reached behind her for the remote control, her insides twisting. Everything had crystalized in her mind the day before. There was no NAFKA, no terrorists; it was France, trying to provoke a war against Germany and get America involved. Tess didn't know why, but she knew it was true. She had known it the moment she saw Guy's face the day before— not stunned, not sad, and not scared, but proud. He had looked proud and satisfied with himself.

When the news came on, at first she couldn't tell what was real and what wasn't. There was the smoldering remains of the French embassy, one corner still standing; a lonesome crag. There were interviews with people covered in dust and debris. They had heard a loud boom and then chaos and screaming as the building collapsed around them. Security camera footage miraculously retrieved from the rubble illustrated their descriptions. Tess wondered if any of it was real. And then what about the people being interviewed, she thought? Were they actors? Was it all animated?

Inevitably the reporters who sat at desks - as opposed to the ones who stood on street corners with microphones at catastrophe scenes - began yammering about the threat from NAFKA, who had claimed responsibility. Photos of the elite of the terrorist group were pinned to the corner of the screen. Tess bit back a guffaw at the satirical skinhead faces, swastikas tattooed to their foreheads and contrived, sinister, squinty eyes with Billy Idol-*esque* raised lips.

Where was the Tess – the pre-Guy Tess - who would never have guessed that the photos were fakes? And yet, she wondered, how was it possible that anyone could look at the other pictures of dust covered corpses, devoid of any blood, even below a severed limb, and not know that they couldn't possibly be real? Was there a doctor watching the news? Tess felt like she was going crazy. To her, the whole thing looked like nothing more than a Hollywood movie set.

But how? How was it possible? She felt sick as the chords of conflict tightened in her gut. Tears born from a feeling of boundless isolation sprung to her eyes as her mother shook her head and tut-tutted. Tess gulped and tried to stay calm.

Then there came footage of the president from the night before, standing at a podium, a row of flags behind him, announcing an alliance with France to bomb NAFKA targets in Germany.

"No," she thought. "No."

Tess was freaking out, she knew. The need to talk to someone - anyone - was becoming an imperative. Was there anyone she could tell, she wondered? No, they would all think she was crazy. There existed only on person she could speak with; who would believe.

She grabbed the phone and went to her bedroom, shutting the door behind her. She waited for her heart to slow down before she dialed Guy's number.

Brave and bright she said, "Are you home? I thought I might come to see you."

Guy hesitated. "I am home, but Yves is here…"

Tess just nodded and hung up. She tugged on a pair of jeans and fished her snow boots out of the closet.

"I have to go out for a little while," she said, clumping towards the living room where the coat closet was. She felt the heat in her face from her mother's surprised stare as she pulled on her parka and grabbed her purse.

Rachel's brows were knitted in confusion. "Tess, darling, what are you talking about? Didn't you hear the mayor? No one's allowed to go out."

Tess smiled brightly, like Tess would do. "I just have to see a friend really quick. I won't be long and it's not far."

She tumbled down the stairs and out the fire door, the cold a smack in her face as she descended into the whitewashed world. Not a soul did she pass as she trudged past the metal gates of the closed storefronts, raising her legs high to plow through the uncleared sidewalks. Not even the distant grind of a snowplow was audible. All was muffled silence, except her breath, hard and timorous with the ragged edges of near-hysteria. By the time she reached Guy's house she was a sweaty mess, but she didn't care.

He jerked open the door, a confused, irritated look on his face. "Tess what is going on? What are you doing here? Yves is at home!"

Tess pushed passed him into the small entrance way. She looked around. "Where is he?"

"He is upstairs, but—"

She looked at him with a forced air of calm purpose. "Can you please tell him to stay there for a few minutes?"

Guy eyed her with a mixture of alarm and something bordering on repulsion, but Tess pushed aside the panic that was rising inside her and forced herself to keep calm as she met his gaze. He opened his mouth to protest but then, as if perceiving her unwavering determination, seemed to change his mind. He exhaled noisily and gripped his hair in annoyance before pounding up the creaky wooden steps, shaking his head and muttering to himself. He was down again in less than a minute.

"Bon," he said, glaring at her. "I told him to stay in his room for a while. Now can you please tell me what is going on?"

Tess trudged wetly into the living room and perched on one of the stiff little chairs. She looked down at the carpet where they had made love once, a long time ago. After a brief pause he followed her, making a big show of recoiling at the puddles she had left and bending over to roll up the cuffs of his jeans. Tess sucked in her lip and released it. She looked at him.

"Did you ever hear of Operation Himmler?" she asked.

Guy was looking at his bare feet, his expression annoyed. Then he looked up at her, hands on his hips. He raised his eyebrows sardonically. "Himmler?"

Tess nodded. She turned away so as not to look at him.

"Yes," she said.

"He was a Nazi, yes?"

Tess raised her eyebrows as if in approval of a student's correct answer. She stared at the fireplace as she spoke.

"Oh yes, that's right. He was a Nazi. You see, the Himmler Project was this plan by Hitler and the other Nazis to create a pretense for Germany to invade Poland. They had a bunch of German prisoners dress up as Polish soldiers and attack a German radio station. Then they used that as precedence for invading Poland."

She felt his eyes boring into her, but she continued to regard the fire-place in front of her with its two-tone brick and glossy carved mantle as if seeing it for the first time.

"Hitler said it was for *lebensraum*—living room, or more space—for the German people. But it was based on a hoax, you see."

She turned and looked at him full in the face. It was a stranger's face, stripped of pretense, wicked and self-satisfied. But she was not afraid.

"A lot of people died from that hoax, and a lot of people are going to die because of this one, aren't they?"

Guy's face resumed its normal, cool veneer. He rolled his eyes and looked down, shaking his head. "Tess, Tess, what on earth are you talking about?"

The anger exploded inside of her like dynamite. She stood up and took a step toward him.

"Don't patronize me, Guy. Don't fucking patronize me." She clenched her fist so hard it vibrated. "I know, okay? I know. I know what you did. I know what you came here for."

She indicated the desk with the computer monitors. "Those aren't for computer games, are they? They're for faking images of terror attacks. That's what you do."

"You are completely insane. *Mon Dieu*, the next thing you will tell me is that the earth is really flat."

Tess clenched her jaw. "I am not crazy. Tell me. Tell me the truth."

"I do not know what you are talking about. Patrick's death—it made you unstuck. You need help, Tess. You need to go see a psychiatrist."

Tess cried, "Oh God!" She shook him by the shoulders, pleading in a harsh whisper. "Please," she said tears streaming down her cheeks, "please tell me. There's never going to be anyone else I can talk to about this. I will be alone with this for the rest of my life. You've *got* to talk to me!"

Slowly but firmly, he grabbed her wrists, lowered her arms, and led her to the door.

He spoke through gritted teeth as they walked. "Yves will want to come downstairs now. You must leave."

He opened the door, and the next thing Tess knew, she was on the other side of it, staring at his severe expression through the glass—the carved cheekbones and firm eyes. She stared back at him, mouth agape, and asked the same question that had consumed her heart with caustic flames after she had unmasked Patrick.

"What made you this way?" She cried.

But his expression remained unchanged. Just a brief shake of the head, and she was dismissed. Slowly, she turned and walked home as hot, angry tears coursed down her cheeks and giant flares of sobs—emitted as bursts of white cloud in the cold air—exploded and echoed in the silence around her.

CHAPTER 27

Yves was not at school the next day. The rest of the class gathered on the rug like they had the morning he first arrived, this time discussing a far more serious anti-French attack.

One of the children, a boy whose family came from Quebec, said, "I heard that in Toronto they were cheering on the streets."

Tess flushed hotly. "I'm sure that's not true. Please, we have to be very careful what we say at times like this."

Out of the corner of her eye, she could see Aleksia roll her eyes before examining her nails.

Another child, a girl named Ariel who always looked like she just tumbled out of bed and into her clothes, called out without raising her hand. "Is there going to be a war? My daddy said there would be."

Tess sighed and repeated the words Karen had instructed them to say. "The important thing to remember is that the adults in your life are going to do everything they can to keep you safe."

Ariel nodded seriously and then shifted her glance around to her classmates, who were also wearing expressions of fear and worry.

It was not difficult, Tess found, to pretend here. Here, in this normal place where everyone believed and accepted what was reported on the news, she did not have to try very hard at all to pretend to be one of them.

Over the next few days, she slipped easily into her old skin. It was only during preps, when she checked Google News and saw updates of the bombing campaign—the accidental death of French or American soldiers or the bombing of a hospital that was mistaken for an armory—that she remembered and shivered, a wave of nausea drifting threateningly to her forehead. In these moments, she felt a loneliness that was almost unbearable and turned to her paperwork, waiting anxiously for the children to return.

Yves did not come back to school. After his third day of absence she casually remarked on the fact to Aleksia, who looked up from her desk when Tess appeared.

"Oh, I forgot to tell you! Yves isn't coming back."

Tess worked to keep her face as still as tree bark. She could not speak.

Aleksia's expression turned to one of delight. "Guy e-mailed me. He's going back to Paris. He's getting married!"

Tess nodded slowly as she accepted the penetration of a sharp knife into her gut. Her eyes moved to the window, where naked tree branches dripped melted snow onto the pedestrians on Smith Street.

"Well, that was sudden," she said soberly.

Aleksia shrugged and laughed lightly. "Maybe she put the screws to him. You know, come back or else..."

Tess nodded and gulped. "Probably."

She shuffled back to her classroom and plopped onto her chair to recover from the blow. There was, she thought, a possibility that Guy really was going back to get married. Who knew? Who could really tell with men like Guy and Patrick? They lied like logs, smooth as polished wood. And if you were naïve enough to think they were good places to rest your body and spirit for a time, you would soon discover that their insides were infested with carpenter bees, which would sting your flesh without mercy.

CHAPTER 28

It was early enough in the day for the skating rink in Prospect Park not to be too busy. The temperature had risen into the upper forties, and the sky was mostly clear. The sun sparkled off the lake on the other side of the rink, and off the ice itself, making sunglasses an imperative.

Molly and her boys careened helplessly into the wall every three or four strokes and Tess took them aside and taught them how to do swizzles and feel their feet in the boots of their skates. Then she drifted to the middle and performed some spins and jumps that made all four children cheer.

Rosie said, "Mommy, I want to learn to do that."

Tess thought of the hours of figure-skating lessons she had endured as a child, and all the hours her mother spent taking her to and from the rink. But she was glad of it, now. She was glad to have something to do that made her feel good.

She said, "I'll get lessons for you, sweetheart."

A little later, she and Molly sipped hot chocolates while the children remained on the ice.

"I hope they think these are coffees," Molly said and laughed.

Tess agreed. "Oh, well, they'll get theirs later."

Molly told her that she and Bill had finally broken up. She tried to shrug it off, but her eyes betrayed her.

"He wanted to get married just as everything between us was getting stale and predictable," she complained. "All I could see was a future of boring routine. I don't know how to explain it, but all of a sudden I realized I didn't want to be married again. I don't want that life back. I want a boy-friend, but I also want *me* time. Anyway, he wants a wife."

She sighed. Tess nodded and offered commiserations. She looked at her friend for a long while to communicate the depths of her understanding. It sucked to be alone. And it sucked to be with someone who sucked.

"There's not a solution that doesn't suck," she said finally.

Molly smiled at her gratefully.

Tess sighed and said, "We'll help one another through this, okay?"

Molly smirked and nodded. Tess looked off in the distance. Would she ever be able to find another man? Could she ever really share an intimate relationship with anyone—male or female—that was 100 percent true and genuine ever again? After a moment Molly reached out to touch her hand.

"Are you okay?" she asked, her eyes squinted with concern. "You seem so far away."

Tess forced a laugh to fend off the tears that always threatened when she thought she was being brave, but then someone offered her a shoulder to cry on. She had already told Molly that Guy left. Now she confessed the part about him getting married as a way to explain the emotions playing out on her face.

Molly looked skeptical. "Are you sure, Tess? Are you sure he didn't just say that as a way of getting to you?"

Tess shrugged. "If he did, it worked."

Molly said tentatively, "You don't want to try and contact him? Maybe you guys need to have one last conversation. You know, for closure."

Closure. Yes, she would really like closure. With Patrick, with Guy…But Patrick was dead and Guy might as well be. When she tried to call his number, an automated recording told her it was no longer in service. His e-mails bounced back as undeliverable, and his Facebook and Twitter accounts had been deleted. Even a Google search for him proved fruitless. He was nowhere to be found and, with a sinking heart, Tess realized she had never taken a picture of him. She wondered how long it would be until she forgot what he looked like altogether.

No, she thought. She would never forget that face. Not ever. It was fixed in her mind's eye forever.

But to Molly she said, "Maybe. That's a good idea."

"I mean, when you're ready…"

Tess nodded in agreement. "Yes, soon."

They came home wet and exhausted. Rachel had decorated the house for Hanukkah in their absence, and the children clapped their hands when they saw the blue and white lights, the tinseled strings of menorahs, dreidels, and presents across the window, and the polished silver menorah on the window sill. Everything was bright and warm and cheerful. Tess felt a swell of nostalgia for her youth and regarded her mother meditatively, remembering the Rachel Shapiro of her childhood and how she thought she had a happy home.

Nothing, she reminded herself, was as it seemed. Nothing.

"Thanks, Mom. Where did you find everything?"

"In the closet in Rosie's room. It was easy to see. They were in clear plastic bags."

The children asked what was for dinner and then went to their rooms to change into dry clothes, charged with excitement for the coming holiday. Tess smiled and went to do the same. She peeled off her jeans and pulled on a pair of cozy gray sweatpants and a flannel shirt and sat on the edge of her bed, staring at her reflection in the mirror above the dresser.

The thought of her mother leaving soon made her feel sad. It was terrible to be alone. Tess felt it now; the weight of a loneliness that would always be with her. The thought of her aging mother living with that feeling all these years made her stomach churn with guilt and depression. She hadn't understood before. A loneliness without respite—forever—was a horrifying prospect.

She sighed and went into the kitchen to fetch the hamburger meat and put the frying pan on the stove to heat up. Her mother came in behind her, and something about her presence forced Tess to turn around. To her horror, Tess saw that her mother was wiping away tears.

Rachel sniffled. "Gee, I'm going to miss you when I go…"

Tess went to her and gave her a quick, tight hug. "Oh, Mom, it's not for ten days!"

Rachel nodded and tried to turn away, but Tess gripped her arm and took a deep breath.

She said, "Mom. Mom, it's okay. I think…I want to come home."

EPILOGUE

Despite the early hour, the first shafts of bright sunlight pierced the windowpanes. Outside, the trees had nearly lost their blossoms, and shiny green leaves sparkled and swayed lazily in the breeze.

Tess stared at them meditatively. Summer in Brooklyn would happen without her and without Sammy and Rosie. Rachel had arranged for them to attend day camp at the Jewish community center in downtown Toronto. They would stay in her apartment while Tess used her free days to search for a home for her and the children and, hopefully, a job.

On the table behind her, surrounded by boxes packed with dishes and kitchen appliances, a bouquet of flowers from her students stood out in contrast to the chaos all around. In ten years, Tess and her family had acquired a mass of personal belongings, and sorting through it all—deciding what to take and what to leave behind—was an arduous task. It reminded Tess of the last weeks of school, when she'd had the children weed through their written work, choose the best example from each month, and then write three ways in which they'd noticed improvement.

Today, she thought, she would start on her own room. It was not an appealing prospect, and a wave of lethargy made her burrow more deeply into her corner spot and stare out over her pulled-up knees broodingly.

She was not thinking of them, but they called to her like a buried heartbeat, long forgotten. Tess slid out of her spot, went to her room, and stood over her chest. It had not been opened in many months, not since Guy. Now, she hesitated, her stomach twisting as she willed herself to pull open the lid. Staring at the neatly stacked collection inside, she was seized by an overwhelming sense of embarrassment for the person who had created it—the person for whom these graphic novels represented a glorified existence and a better person.

Silently, she turned and padded back to the kitchen to fetch a garbage bag from the box on the counter. Back in her room, she grabbed handfuls of the manuscripts, without stopping to look at them, and pushed them frenziedly into the trash bag.

It was so full by the time she was done, she thought she could have used two bags instead of one, but she reached inside and shifted the contents around so everything fit before tying the short ends into a tiny but firm knot. She was perspiring as she dragged it out of her room behind her, like a hidden corpse.

As she passed Sammy's room, she heard the springs of his bed creak and his body slide out of bed.

"What are you doing?" he asked sleepily, rubbing his eyes as he stood framed in his doorway.

Tess opened her mouth and shut it. "I'm just getting an early start on packing. I'll be right back."

She opened the door and made her way down the long hallway to the trash room, dragging her load. Corners of pages had poked their way through the black plastic by the time she arrived there, as if trying to escape. She yanked open the chute door and heaved the bag into the narrow opening, shoving it in until it broke past the initial box and swooshed down the dark tunnel.

She stared after it, heart pounding, breath coming in jagged pants. After a moment she stood up straight and swallowed, searching herself for a sense of emptiness or loss. But those feelings were already a part of her, and she realized that pretending to be someone else was no longer an indulgence; it was a fact of life. She no longer needed to pretend to be Andrea Chambers to escape being Tess. She just needed to pretend to be Tess.